THE DEVIL'S
PROMISE

Veronica Bennett was an English lecturer for many years, but now writes full-time. In 2011, she was elected a Hawthornden Fellow, and spent four weeks at the International Writers' Retreat at Hawthornden Castle, Scotland. "I worked on other books while I was there," she says, "but the atmosphere and setting of Hawthornden made such an impression that I decided to set my next historical novel in a Scottish castle. What happens in the book is imaginary, of course, but without my stay at a real castle I would never have envisaged the fictional one. I am grateful to Mrs Drue Heinz and the Hawthornden Foundation for making *The Devil's Promise* possible." Veronica lives in Middlesex with her husband, and has an adult son and daughter.

Books by the same author

Angelmonster

The Boy-free Zone

Cassandra's Sister

Fish Feet

Monkey

Shakespeare's Apprentice

Vice and Virtue

For younger readers

Dandelion and Bobcat

The *Poppy Love* series

THE DEVIL'S PROMISE

VERONICA
BENNETT

**WALKER
BOOKS**

This is a work of fiction. Names, characters, places and incidents
are either the product of the author's imagination or, if real, used
fictitiously. All statements, activities, stunts, descriptions, information
and material of any other kind contained herein are included for
entertainment purposes only and should not be relied on for
accuracy or replicated as they may result in injury.

First published 2013 by Walker Books Ltd
87 Vauxhall Walk, London SE11 5HJ

2 4 6 8 10 9 7 5 3 1

Text © 2013 Veronica Bennett
Cover illustration © 2013 Adam McCauley

The right of Veronica Bennett to be identified as author of this work has been
asserted by her in accordance with the Copyright, Designs and Patents Act 1988.

This book has been typeset in M Bembo and Stuyvesant ICG.

Printed and bound in Great Britain by Clays Ltd, St Ives plc

British Library Cataloguing in Publication Data:
a catalogue record for this book is available from the British Library

ISBN 978-1-4063-4323-6

www.walker.co.uk

In memory of my mother,
Margaret Hyndman May
(1919–1985)

PART ONE

THE FAERIE
CAT

1889

Silence. Dead silence.

The silence was all around them. No birds sang; there was no wind. Here in this desolate place, it seemed to her that even the weather had ceased to be. The sky was white, a blank canvas. No rain fell; no sun shone. There was only death.

She stepped forward. Faint with fear, nauseated by grief, she stood beside the grave for a long time, cradling the almost weightless bundle. The silence was so intense she could almost touch it. She turned quickly, seized by dread. But the man had not abandoned her. There he stood, not looking at her, his pale face shadowed beneath the trees.

"It is time," he said.

Slowly she knelt down. She slid the baby's swaddled body from her arms into the waiting earth. As she did so she felt his head loll backwards on his tiny neck, as if it still held life.

She began to weep, her stricken sobs piercing the air while the man shovelled soil into the hole, firmed it with his foot and covered it with sodden leaves, handful after handful until all sign of the disturbance of the earth had disappeared.

Exhausted now, she knelt silently, but she did not listen to his prayer. Her ears were assailed by screams. Inhuman screams. First one, then more and more crows darted between the trees and settled nearby. Their ragged feathers and glittering eyes were repellent to her, a vision of horror.

"This place is cursed," she told the man. "I will never return here."

The man's gaze did not shift from the grave. His voice was a whisper. "Neither will I." He wiped his hands on his handkerchief and shouldered the shovel. "We will never again pay respects at our son's grave."

"What need is there to pay respects?" she asked. "Our son is not dead."

DUTY & DIGNITY

1910, twenty-one years later

I was melting. My corset constricted my ribs, and the pins that skewered my new hat dug into my scalp. My navy serge skirt was too thick for such a warm spring day, but it was the only garment I possessed that my mother considered sober enough. Over the skirt and my buttoned-up silk blouse, my best wool coat – velvet-collared and cuffed, with a vent at the back and polished bone buttons – enclosed me as airlessly as a pot encloses simmering soup. Slowly, but definitely, I was cooking.

Until now, the only hats I had owned were straw ones. I liked the one with the tipped-back brim, but the boater with the mustard-coloured ribbons of St Giles's College was hideous. Perhaps, now I'd left the school for ever, my mother would let me throw not only the hat, but the entire uniform, into the dustbin. Especially since I had my first grown-up, plain felt hat. A hat that a women, not a schoolgirl, would wear for an occasion such as this. An occasion that demanded mourning clothes.

*You would have allowed the hurling away of the mustard uni-
form, and laughed while I did it, wouldn't you, Father?*

My throat ached. I swallowed, twice. It went on aching.

So unexpected, people had exclaimed. *A man in his prime*,
they had murmured. *Our deepest condolences*, they had written.
But all I could think of was the fact that he was dead, whatever anyone said or wrote or did. And his love – unwavering,
affectionate, true – had died with him. He had taken it with
him wherever he had gone, and it was no longer in the world.
Other people loved me, of course. But no one inspired me as
Father did to love them as much in return.

I forced myself to go on thinking about hats and how hot
I was. I must not let the tears fall. Mother, though as bereft
as I was, had instructed me in the conduct she expected at
the church, and afterwards at the graveside. "Dignity," she had
insisted. "We may weep in private, or with friends of our station. But people *not* of our station will come to pay their
respects to your father today, and in front of *them* we must
remain composed."

I hadn't troubled myself to question her judgement.
I knew from experience what the answer would be: "It is our
duty, my dear." Father was important; the Grahams were the
first family of the district; convention must be served.

Farm and factory workers, servants, shopkeepers from
Gilchester, Mr Goddard the bank manager and our family
lawyer, Mr Haines, were gathered in St Stephen's church to
hear Reverend Baxter. And as the mourners followed the

coffin to the grave-plot in the churchyard, the crowd grew even greater. I saw people I recognized, but many more I did not. Even one of the four pall-bearers – a well-dressed man, neatly bearded beneath his top hat – was a stranger to me. The other three were Jarvis, who had been our butler since before I was born, Mr Groves the factory foreman, and the undertaker's assistant. Father had no brothers, and his dearest friend, an army officer who had been best man at his wedding, had been killed in action ten years ago.

The coffin was lowered to its rest. I held tightly to my mother's arm, only half-hearing the vicar intoning the burial prayer and scattering soil on the coffin lid. It was final. Father was gone. Mother and I, Chester House, Graham's Wholesome Foods and all that went with them remained.

I did not weep. Duty and dignity prevailed. Jarvis stood grim-faced between Mrs Jamison, the housekeeper, and Mr Napier, the head gardener. I knew that every one of them was thinking the same thing: *now that Mrs Graham is a widow and there is no male heir, Miss Catriona will inherit the estate and the business. But she cannot be mistress of such a legacy alone, so our future lies in the hands of a man no one has yet seen or heard of – Miss Catriona's future husband.*

This knowledge made me uncomfortable, though I knew the truth of it. But there was another truth the servants did not know. I did not *want* to inherit Chester House and its servants, and Graham's Wholesome Foods and its workers. I did not want to be the most important woman in Gilchester.

In particular, I did not want to marry a man attracted by the prospect of this inheritance. Such a man, I was certain, would never claim my affection. I had loved my father, and the turnout in the churchyard was evidence of his fairness towards his employees and the respect he commanded from his friends. But my choice of husband was my own, and I would exercise it.

The burial was over. Mother turned from the graveside, and led the way down the hill to the waiting carriages. I was still clasping her arm. All around us, other mourners moved too, conversing in murmurs, bowing their heads as they passed the grave. Susan, my mother's maid, had her handkerchief at her eyes. Mr Napier blew his nose. Someone was speaking in my ear – Mr Haines, I thought – but I did not comprehend his words. There seemed to be a mist around me. I could not see where I was stepping. I stumbled; someone caught me around the waist.

"Um…" I heard myself begin. Then the mist thickened, and there was only darkness.

"Give her air, if you please."

When I opened my eyes, I found myself lying on the carriage seat with my head on Mother's lap. Opposite us sat the stranger in the top hat.

"I am a doctor," he said. "You fainted, that is all. And who can be surprised, in this heat?" He lifted his hat to the crowd who surrounded the open carriage, trying each to suggest helpful remedies and stop the others from doing so. "Ladies and gentlemen, Miss Graham is perfectly well, but needs to go home. Stand back, if you will, and let the driver start."

They obeyed, though with suspicion. Then I heard the "Hup!", the wheels crunched on the gravel, and the carriage rumbled forward. "Oh!" I exclaimed, sitting up. "My hat!" It had been removed, and tendrils of my hair had slid free of their pins. "Where is it?"

"It is here by me, quite safe," Mother reassured me. "How do you feel, my dear?"

"Foolish."

"No need," said the man. He held out his hand. "We have not been introduced. I am Hamish Buchanan, your late father's cousin."

"Father's cousin? I never knew—"

"Doctor Buchanan was unknown to us all before this morning," said Mother. "He sent a note to the house before we went to church, but I must have forgotten to mention it to you. I was distracted. It is a relief," she sighed, "to have the funeral service over."

"I arrived late anyway, after my long journey from Scotland," said Doctor Buchanan, "so I sidled in at the back." He was not quite smiling, but there was an amiable light in his eye. His voice had a Scottish lilt that gave it a homely sound. Perhaps, as a doctor, he presented what was called a good "bedside manner". But even if it *was* a manner, I liked it.

"Then thank you for coming all this way," I said, "and for looking after me."

"Yes, indeed," said Mother hurriedly. "We are indebted to you." Turning her profile to the doctor, she rested her gloved hand on the side of the carriage. "Especially," she added, shooting him a glance from the shadow of her hat brim, "since we had never heard of any Scottish cousin of David's before today."

Doctor Buchanan interwove his fingers on the silver top of the cane he held between his knees. He observed Mother closely, his face alternately in sun and shadow as the carriage passed the line of elms that bordered the drive to Chester House. "I will be happy to explain," he said, "when we are indoors and Miss Graham has a cup of sweet tea in her hand."

"Oh, 'Catriona', please!" cried Mother, turning once more to face him. "There is no need to stand on ceremony with her – she is only seventeen!"

The doctor frowned slightly, perhaps wondering what, if anything, the one had to do with the other. "Very well," he agreed. "Then you and your daughter must call me Doctor Hamish, as everyone in Drumwithie does, including my patients."

"Doctor Hamish," Mother repeated with satisfaction. The jet decorations on her hat quivered as she tilted her head enquiringly. "Hamish is a Scottish name, I believe?"

"Indeed it is."

"And so is Catriona," she told him authoritatively. "It is the Gaelic form of Catherine."

Doctor Hamish looked at me. "Well, Catriona, you have something of David in the setting of your eyes. His were blue, of course, but the expression is there." Then he took his attention back to my mother. "The family's Scottish descent influenced your choice of name for your daughter, I think?"

"Oh, yes!" Mother assured him. "David often said he wanted to find out more about his Scottish relatives, but he never seemed to get round to it. He was a very busy man, you must understand. Anyway, we both liked the name Catriona, and there are so many Mabels and Dorothys these days, we wished to be a little different from the crowd. My name, however," she added, "is very English. I am called Rose. Please, do use it, doctor."

"Very well," said Doctor Hamish, rather stiffly. "Rose it is."

I reached across and picked up my hat. "Mother, we are here."

"Already? I shall lead the way!" she declared, gathering her skirt.

I followed more slowly. My legs felt shaky, and I was pleased to take Doctor Hamish's arm, promptly offered. My stiff skirt slapped my ankles as we approached the house. "Thank you," I said softly. "I don't usually faint, you know. I am unnaturally robust, Mother says."

He smiled, but said nothing. Mother was in the open doorway, organizing. "We would like tea in private in the library," she called to Jarvis as he and Mrs Jamison hurried up the drive. "Show everyone else to the dining room and make my apologies. We will join them when Miss Graham is fully recovered. And, Mrs Jamison," she added to the housekeeper, "will you make the guest room ready for Doctor Buchanan?"

"But there is no need!" protested the doctor. "I can put up at the inn in the High Street. I must return to Scotland tomorrow."

Mother's shoulders straightened. "I insist you stay with us. It is the least we can do."

"In that case, I am extremely grateful for your hospitality."

We settled ourselves in the library armchairs, surrounded by Father's books and shaded against the westering sun by parchment blinds.

"I hope my housekeeper is quick with the tea!" exclaimed Mother, removing her gloves. "I must confess I am fatigued, though not, I might add, to the point of fainting."

"Mother, it was not *fatigue* that overcame me." Grief surged up; I could not say more.

Doctor Hamish looked from me to my mother, and back again at me. "Are you feeling better now?" he asked.

I nodded, and murmured my thanks.

"Catriona is never indisposed for long." Mother smoothed her skirt, her eyes on the doctor's face. "Now, Doctor Hamish," she said in a businesslike way. "I am very interested in finding out why David never introduced us to you. You said you would tell us when we were indoors, and here we are."

"The explanation is quite simple," replied the doctor calmly. "Long ago, before either of us had met our future wives, your husband and I suffered an estrangement. I cannot tell you the reason for it – that has gone with him to his grave, and must remain there – but I have long regretted the loss of his acquaintance. It is too late now to renew it, of course, but when I read the notice of his death in *The Times*, I resolved to attend his funeral."

There was a short silence. It struck me that so far there was nothing to prove this man spoke the truth. He could be an impostor who had read the announcement in *The Times* and set out to try his luck. Mother and I had both warmed to him, but perhaps, I decided bleakly, the ability to be charming is a vital quality of the charlatan.

"It is very pleasant," continued Mother, "to discover a new branch of the family. I wonder that David never mentioned you to us."

"The estrangement was such that he would not have done so," said the doctor solemnly. "It was over twenty years ago, and concerned a personal matter which he would not wish me to disclose, even now."

"Such a pity!" exclaimed Mother. Her tone was light, but I knew this artlessness was a pretence. Her eyes showed me that she was every bit as suspicious as I was. "Tell me, is anyone else in the family aware of what took place?"

"No one knew of it," said the doctor crisply. He looked up as the door opened. "Ah, tea!"

Jarvis placed the tray, bowed and left. The sandwiches, scones and fruitcake did not tempt me, but I accepted the cup of tea my mother handed me. "Of course," she said as she passed Doctor Hamish his own tea, "David was a Graham, and my mother-in-law's family – also Scottish – are called Hamilton. So as a Buchanan, how do you fit in?"

"Through my mother, who was a Graham. She and David's father were sister and brother. May I?" He took a sandwich and bit into it with enthusiasm. When he had swallowed, he added, "I always called him Uncle Peter, though I believe his first name was Ernest. His wife, David's mother, was called Eleanor. David used to refer to them, in private of course, as 'The Es'."

Mother smiled. "Indeed he did. And of course, Granny and Grandpa were very well aware of it, weren't they, Catriona?" Not waiting for my reply, she continued. "But I wonder that my father-in-law never mentioned you, Doctor. You are his blood nephew, the son of his only sister, after all."

Doctor Hamish chewed his sandwich thoughtfully for a moment. "That is true. But an estrangement such as ours severed all family relationship, so irrevocably that David's parents could not maintain correspondence with mine." He sighed lightly, wiping his mouth on his napkin. "And a mere few months after the rift, my dear mother died, ending all connection with the Grahams. Neither her brother nor his wife attended her funeral."

"Oh! I am very sorry to hear that!"

I hoped the doctor did not detect the relief in Mother's voice. She was evidently convinced that he was genuine. But I was not. "Mm ... but I suppose you know all about my father's Uncle Augustus and the shipwreck, Doctor Hamish?" I asked solemnly. "What is your opinion of what really happened? Was the captain to blame?"

They looked at me, nonplussed. "I'm afraid I..." began Doctor Hamish. "Er ... I have never heard of Uncle Augustus."

"Neither have I." I sipped my tea. "He does not exist."

He was surprised for an instant, then he grinned, and reached for another sandwich. "Here be a braw scholar, ye ken," he said in an exaggerated Scottish accent. "A' must watch ma' p's and q's!"

"Oh, yes," said Mother, with an approving glance at me. "Catriona may be dark, when David was so fair, but her mind is just like her father's – sharp as a pin!"

Throughout this exchange the doctor had been studying me. I was not looking at him, but I could sense his eyes following my movements as I reached for a piece of bread and butter. I had no appetite, but I knew that if I ate nothing Mother would fuss.

"Please, Doctor," I said, almost before I had fully decided to speak, "may I ask a question?"

"Of course."

"Why, after so many years of estrangement from Father, have you approached us so unexpectedly upon his death?"

Mother looked at me in horror. "Catriona!" she cried, with a sideways glance at Doctor Hamish, whose face had coloured, "consider your words, do!"

Mystified for a second, I suddenly understood how my meaning might be misconstrued. "Oh!" I put my hand over my mouth, aghast. "Of course I did not mean… Forgive me…"

"Do not distress yourself," said the doctor, smiling his almost-smile. "I came because by attending David's funeral I hoped to make myself known to his family, and, I suppose, make some sort of peace with him in death that I could not make in life. I am aware he left you and your mother very well provided for, but you need not fear that I seek any sort of bequest." He turned his attention to Mother. "Except, if you would consent to it, Rose, a small token of my cousin's life? A photograph, perhaps, or some memento such as a snuff box? David and I were close as children. I would dearly love something to remember him by."

"Of course." Mother rose and opened the top drawer of the library desk. "Would you like to have this?"

The doctor took the silver cigarette case she held out. "I remember this!" he said in amazement. "David had it when he was quite young, before we… Are you sure you are willing to part with it?"

"Perfectly sure. Everything that was David's is mine now, so it is in my gift. Please take it, and think of him every time you use it."

I was familiar with the cigarette case too. It had been a gift from Granny and Grandpa when Father had gone up to Cambridge in 1886. In honour of the family's Scottish heritage, it was embossed with a thistle design, enamelled in blue.

"You are most generous," said the doctor, clearly moved by the gift. "Indeed, this makes me even more determined to make up for lost time." He turned to me. "Catriona, if you have no objection, may I suggest something? A plan which may be of interest to you."

I still felt flustered after my faux pas. "A plan?" I repeated uncertainly.

"Let me explain," he said, with a glance at Mother. "During my journey from Scotland I had time to consider many things, about both the past and the future. I was nervous, I confess, about meeting David's wife and daughter. I thought you might resent my sudden appearance, after so many years."

Mother hurried to reassure him. "Oh, no, indeed, we are more than happy to see you."

"I understand that now," continued the doctor, "and I am relieved, and touched, by the warmth of your welcome."

She bowed; I kept my eyes on the doctor's face. His homely manner had not changed, but there was urgency in his expression. "As I sat there on the train, with memories of my childhood with David going through my head," he said, "I realized that although I could no longer do anything for him—"

"But you *have!*" interrupted Mother. "You have come all this way to honour his passing!"

The doctor nodded. "Very well, but it would ease my conscience greatly if you would allow me to do something else, for those David has left behind." His gaze slid towards me. "Especially for Catriona."

"For Catriona?" echoed Mother faintly, her teacup halfway to her mouth. "What can you mean, Doctor?"

"Merely that I have long regretted David's absence from a place he once loved. As a child, he loved to spend holidays at Drumwithie. He never returned there in adult life, and he can never go there now, but, Catriona" – he looked earnestly into my face – "would you consider returning to Scotland with me, and spending the summer at Drumwithie Castle?"

No one spoke. Until this moment I had faced the prospect of a summer spent in an atmosphere of deep mourning, with a fretful mother and the gloom of uncertainty hanging over the affairs of Graham's Wholesome Foods. Now I was no longer a schoolgirl, Mother would soon present me to Gilchester's social circle, while overseeing the business and indulging in her favourite occupation, horseriding. This interim between my leaving school and getting married was an inconvenience for both her and me. But now Doctor Hamish had offered me a lifeline. Going to Drumwithie promised a few weeks of fresh fields, freedom from Gilchester gossips and, tantalizingly, new acquaintances.

I glanced at Mother; her gaze was on Doctor Hamish's

face, a bemused enquiry in her eyes. "Goodness me, are you sure?" she asked. "This is very kind of you… I think it can only do Catriona good, to see a little of the world. But she is not the easiest of girls, you know, with whom to maintain … er, calm communication. She has ideas."

"I should very much hope so," replied Doctor Hamish stoutly. "Indeed, she reminds me of my son, Jamie. Quick, observant, scornful of pretention and feebleness, yet with the makings of a gentleman. Or in this case, a lady."

Mother was interested. "You have a son? Of Catriona's age?"

"A little older. He is twenty-one, and beginning to find his way in the world. It is sometimes difficult for him…" He paused, and considered the carpet, with the look of a man concentrating on the careful selection of his words. "Drumwithie is a small, old-fashioned place, though it does have a railway station. The castle itself is isolated and our circle rather restricted." He smiled bleakly. "I am sure Jamie would say it is old-fashioned too. He has no idea of Catriona's existence, and I have no doubt he will be very pleased to discover it."

Mother's enquiring look became one of intense interest. "Has the boy not been away to school, then?"

The doctor shook his head. "There is no day school nearby, and it was his mother's wish that he be educated at home."

"Ah. And your wife's name is…?"

"Anne." He paused, then added, "She is away from Drumwithie at present, and is unlikely to return for some time."

"I see," said Mother, though it was plain from her expression that she did not. "So … is your son to attend the University?"

Doctor Hamish considered this for a few moments, still seeking his words with care. "I hope he will enter the Medical School at the University of Edinburgh next term," he said at last. "It has taken him several attempts to gain the necessary qualifications."

I knew exactly what Mother was about to say, and she said it.

"But he has got there in the end, however twisting the path, and that is the important thing!" She picked up her teacup and took several small sips. I could tell by her rapid blinking that her brain was busy. "Catriona has been very well educated too, at St Giles's College, you know. But the girls there do not generally go on to university." She sat forward and added, "Now, would you like more tea, Doctor Hamish? Or another sandwich?"

The doctor seemed not to hear. He was regarding me calmly. "So, Catriona, what do you say? Would you like to come to Drumwithie?"

"Very much, if Mother can spare me."

"Of course I can spare you!" Mother put down her cup. "What do I ever do here, that I cannot do without you?"

26

"Then that is settled," said Doctor Hamish. "Today is Friday. Is tomorrow morning too soon to leave? I have patients I must attend to."

I could not protest, though tomorrow *did* seem rather soon. But Mother was enthusiastic. "Of course not! Your work is important, Doctor, and Catriona's things can be packed in a trice. She is not a fussy child."

"In that case," he added to me, "I will telegraph to Jamie to expect us tomorrow evening. There is a train at seven thirty in the morning to Birmingham, where we can join the London–Edinburgh train."

"Very well," said Mother. "Susan and Edith will make a start on the packing after the funeral people have gone. Mrs Jamison will have to spare them from the clearing up."

I heard strain in her voice and glanced at her face. Her smile was tight and the expression of her eyes unconnected to it. In the twelve days since Father's death, it had been Mother's responsibility to deal with the local doctor, the undertaker, the registry, the bank, the solicitor, the vicar and an apparently endless stream of correspondence. All I had done was follow what instructions I was given and keep out of the way. Today had been long and anxious, and was not yet over.

"Mother, why not go to your guests now?" I suggested. "I am feeling much better, and when Doctor Hamish has had his tea, I will bring him to the dining room."

She wavered, glancing from me to the doctor and back. Then she nodded, took two sips of tea and replaced her cup on the tray. "Very well. You are quite right, no one can go home until I have made my rounds of them, and I must confess I am very ready for them to depart!" She got to her feet and adjusted her skirt. "Do I look all right?" she asked me.

"You look pale, but it becomes you."

This was what she liked to hear. I watched her take polite leave of the doctor and make her way out of the room, her skirt swishing on the polished floor of the library. A wave of affection rushed over me. Poor Mother! She was but thirty-eight years old. A long widowhood awaited her.

"There is no need for you to stay with me if you wish to lie down," said Doctor Hamish, brushing crumbs from his lap. "I am perfectly content. These sandwiches are delicious."

"In the dining room you may have cold beef, pies, cheeses, trifle, jellies… You can imagine the trouble Mother has gone to."

"Indeed." He paused. I knew he was looking at me, but was not yet composed enough to look at him. "Your mother is a remarkable woman and very worthy of her husband."

The tears came. Some fell into the tea, and some onto the front of my blouse. Most ran down my cheeks and dripped off the end of my chin. Duty and dignity forgotten, I began to sob.

The doctor gently took away my cup and saucer. "My dear," he said, "weep all you wish. Grief is best expressed, you know. I will go and join your mother now. She deserves my assistance, as a member of the family."

I nodded, hardly noticing him stand up. As he passed my chair he put a hand on my shoulder. "You had no need to doubt my sincerity, my dear, though I understand why you did. But I promise I will do anything within my power to make up for this long estrangement." I felt him squeeze my shoulder gently, then his hand dropped away. "Now, you had better go and lie down, and forget about social niceties," he told me. "There will be plenty of time tomorrow to make each other's better acquaintance. Drumwithie is a long journey away."

I could not raise my head to thank him. When he had shut the library door behind him, I wept until my handkerchief was sodden. Then, as the torrent passed, I became aware of sounds from the dining room: glasses and crockery, chattering voices, even laughter. The reason for a funeral, Mother had explained, was to allow people release from anxiety. With a drink in their hand, they could begin to think of life instead of death.

I roused myself, sniffing and hiccupping, and pushed myself out of the chair. Was Doctor Hamish one of the chatterers? He had taken the corner of the coffin as naturally as if he and Father had been brothers, not estranged cousins. We had only met him for the first time an hour ago, yet he was "assisting" Mother as if he, as well as she, were hosting the funeral reception.

And within a few hours I would be on a train, travelling northwards with this affable stranger, to a place my father had once loved. Drumwithie Castle. Its name sounded exotic, different from any word I had ever heard. As I climbed the stairs, I comforted myself with the thought that whatever awaited me there, and whatever the reason behind the cousins' estrangement, Father would approve.

THE BONNIEST CAT
IN SCOTLAND

Our journey to Edinburgh was exhausting.

"Why does sitting in a train all day make you so tired?" I asked the doctor. "Surely you should arrive at your destination refreshed, when you haven't been walking, or cycling, or doing anything but watch the countryside go by?"

He smiled at me from the seat opposite. "I'm afraid I have no medical explanation for the phenomenon. But at least we are almost there." He leaned forward, the better to see out of the window. "Look," he said eagerly, "we are passing through the city. Have you ever seen such a black and filthy place?"

The last of the sunlight gilded the highest rooftops, but Edinburgh did indeed look dirty. Smoke hung in the air, and the buildings were old and, as the doctor had said, black. The lumpy shape of Castle Rock rose out of the gloom. It looked grim and unwelcoming.

"Edinburgh is known affectionately as 'Auld Reekie'," said Doctor Hamish, standing to reach up for our luggage.

"Or 'Old Smoky' in English. You can see why, eh?"

I do not know what I answered; at that moment the engine whistled so piercingly I had to cover my ears. We were drawing into the station, accompanied by a cacophony of hissing and chuffing. Then there was the unloading of my trunk and the doctor's Gladstone bag, the handing-down onto the platform, the sounds of Scottish voices, hastening boots and the cries of weary children. Doctor Hamish led me towards the iron bridge that crossed the railway lines. "We have only six minutes to catch the connecting train, so if you would be pleased to make haste, my dear…"

I quickened my stride, but it was hard to keep up with him. "How long are we going to be on *this* train?" I asked breathlessly.

"We shall be at Drumwithie Station at …" – he consulted his fob watch as we boarded the train – "five past nine. Jamie will meet us and we shall be at the castle by half past."

My fatigue had almost got the better of me. It was soaking through to my bones, glueing my body to the seat. And I was further weakened by hunger. It was nearly eight hours since we had taken luncheon in the restaurant car of the Edinburgh train, and I had eaten only a few biscuits with my tea at four o'clock. I had no strength for conversation; I heard and saw no more until I was awakened by the halting of the train and Doctor Hamish's hand on my arm. "Wake up, my dear," he murmured. "We are here."

I half stepped, half stumbled into the near-darkness. The

only sound was the hissing of the engine; the platform seemed to float amongst trees, vertical banks of evergreens lining each side of the track. The sky had turned the violet-blue of dusk, and the shadows were so black they seemed solid. I shuddered. The silence and gloom of the place were profound.

When the steam cleared I saw a lantern moving in the half-light. Someone was approaching from the road. Doctor Hamish led me through the little gate. The person with the lantern came near enough for it to illuminate his face clearly. And that was the moment when I first set eyes on James McAllister Buchanan.

He came closer. The light showed a striking face – youthful, with prominent bones. His eyes, set deep, looked at me with a penetrating gaze. He was dressed informally in a light canvas jacket and a shirt with no collar. His hair flopped forward over his brow, as bright gold as a new sovereign. I marvelled, wondering if it was the artificial light that made it appear so radiant. Then I found my hand gripped and my arm pumped in an enthusiastic handshake.

"Miss Catriona Graham!" He had the same Scottish intonation as his father, though his voice was higher-pitched. "Heigh-ho, I will call you Cat! And I believe you to be the bonniest cat in Scotland!"

I intended to speak, but no words came out. I must have been gaping like a goldfish, because I heard Doctor Hamish's low laugh. "Do not be alarmed," he murmured in my ear.

"We have learnt to humour him." Then, louder, "Now, Jamie, this trunk will not shift itself."

Jamie grinned, uttered a sound something like "Ha-iyya!", gave his father the lantern, hoisted my trunk onto his shoulder and followed us to the waiting carriage. It was an old one-horse trap, open to the warmth of the evening. I accepted Doctor Hamish's helping hand and stepped up, amused to imagine my mother's expression had *she* been presented with such a vehicle. At home we had a brougham, pulled by our two most presentable horses. But in Gilchester there were tree-lined lanes and paved streets. Here, in this wild and wooded landscape, a fast, well-sprung brougham, with two trotting bays tossing their heads, would be absurd.

I settled myself on the bench seat, with the doctor opposite and the luggage between us on the straw-strewn floor. Jamie put on his cap, climbed into the driving seat and took up the reins. "Cat, meet Kelpie," he said amiably, indicating the elderly looking pony.

"Pleased to make your acquaintance, Kelpie," I said obediently.

Jamie laughed. "See her ears turning? She knows her name."

"We shall be at the castle in fifteen minutes," said Doctor Hamish, leaning forward to put the lantern in the holder. "Half past nine was an accurate estimation."

"And how my father *loves* an accurate estimation!" came Jamie's voice.

It was too dark to see the doctor's expression, and he said nothing. I gripped the edge of the trap as Kelpie stepped forward. Her shoes rang on tarmacked road for a few yards, but then became thuds as the ground softened. The way to the castle appeared to be along a narrow track, scattered with sand in its muddier parts. From what I could see in the limited light, it was bordered by shrubby trees and an ancient fence, which shortly gave way to the impenetrable blackness of a forest. Trees stretched away on both sides, their branches sometimes encroaching far enough on the road for the pony to swerve.

"Watch out for the deer, Jamie," warned Doctor Hamish. "You are driving a little fast."

"If you wish me to get us back by half past nine, Father, then I had better drive as fast *as your accurate estimation* requires!" retorted Jamie.

The doctor ignored Jamie's remark, choosing instead to lean across and ask me if I was warm enough.

"Quite warm enough, thank you," I told him. He was about to sit back, but I continued quickly, before I lost courage. "I must say, though, we *are* travelling rather quickly."

"Hah!" cried Jamie, pulling on the reins. "For *you*, Miss Bonniest-Cat-in-Scotland, I will slow down. And I hope the deer and my father are thankful."

We were silent the rest of the way. I breathed the pine-scented air, relieved to be freed from the stuffy railway carriage, and increasingly excited about seeing Drumwithie. The trap jolted as the uneven road wound uphill and the trees thinned out. Then, as suddenly as if an invisible hand had drawn a line, they disappeared altogether. As we breasted the hill, I felt as if I had stepped off the edge of the world, so dense was the blackness all around us. Ahead I could just make out two low stone pillars. Jamie slowed the horse while we cleared the narrow passage between them, and then we began the final ascent to the castle.

Doctor Hamish had told me that the castle was built high in order to see and repel the approach of hostile clansmen in ancient times. But I had not taken in that it was built on a rock, which rose against the night sky like a stooping giant. The building itself seemed to grow out of the granite like a natural thing, its walls thick with vegetation. Swaying towards it through the dark, with the rumble of the wheels and the clopping of the horse's hooves filling my ears, I was transfixed.

The place was both older and newer than I had imagined. A ruined tower rose at one corner, but the inhabited part of the house was oblong, with a tiled roof, a large collection of chimneys, polished casement windows and an arched door studded with nails. It looked like a bigger version of the manor house belonging to our local Gilchester squire. But as we drew nearer, I saw that there was no similarity between the pasture that surrounded the squire's house and the situation of the castle.

Drumwithie's grandeur was in its setting. The approach to the front door was by means of a narrow stone bridge, separated from the chasm of blackness below by a low, moss-covered wall. I clutched the side of the trap. On all sides, the land fell away from the house. Save for a strip of gravel and lawn beside the carriage sweep, it was supported by nothing but rock. The building looked as if it had been dropped from the heavens, to settle comfortably on the highest point of the landscape.

There was little moonlight to show the magnificence of the place, yet I sensed it. When we drew to a halt at the door, I turned to Doctor Hamish, fired with admiration. "This must be one of the most beautiful situations in Scotland!" I exclaimed. "How proud you must be to live here!"

He smiled diffidently. "Humble, rather than proud, my dear. Jamie is very attached to it."

I waited for Jamie to acknowledge his father's comment, but he was silent as he jumped down, unbolted the back of the trap and took hold of my trunk. I stole a glance at his face; his mouth was firmly set, but the expression in his eyes, shaded by the peak of his cap, was hidden from me.

Though there were lights each side of the castle door, Doctor Hamish took the carriage-lantern from its holder. "Watch your step, now," he warned, holding it above my head. "Will you take my hand?"

I took it gratefully and stepped down from the trap. Jamie preceded us with my trunk into the vestibule, then turned back for his father's suitcase. The two men did not look at each other. I felt anxious; what had caused this coldness between them?

When Doctor Hamish opened the door that led from the vestibule to the main hall, I saw only a long, vaulted room with a stone floor and a log fire at the far end. "We call this the Great Hall, because that is what it has always been called," he said. "We use it as a sort of drawing room."

At first I thought the room was empty. But then I heard the rustle of petticoats. A lady rose from a chair by the fire and turned to face us. My first impression was of a tall figure – not young, but erect, elegantly dressed, and with the demeanour of a person who considers herself important. She did not step forward, but waited for us to approach and offered me her hand.

"Good evening, Miss Graham," she said, with no welcoming smile on her lips. "I am Jean McAllister, Doctor Hamish's mother-in-law. I trust you have had a pleasant journey?"

"Yes, thank you."

"Our countryside is beautiful, is it not?"

"Yes, indeed."

"And the city of Edinburgh stands comparison with Rome, or Athens, does it not?"

I hesitated; I had not been to Rome or Athens. What did this lady wish me to say?

"Have a heart, Grandmother!" cried Jamie, banging the door behind him. "There will be plenty of time to advertise the attractions of Scotland to Cat when she has had her supper!" He threw his cap onto a chair and sprawled on a small sofa, looking at us from under his flap of hair. "And talking of supper, if there's any to spare, I am ready for it. Where's Bridie?"

"Heating up the broth," replied his grandmother. She sat down again in her chair and adjusted her skirt. "She will have heard you arrive." She tilted her head in my direction. "Miss Graham, have you given my grandson permission to call you by that ludicrous name?"

"She did not need to give me permission," said Jamie. He held his hair back with one hand and contemplated me, his eyes glittering. There was enough light now for me to see that they were an unusual colour, a bright sea-green, speckled like robins' eggs. "It is obvious I must call her Cat. Is it not, Cat?"

"Jamie!" His grandmother rapped the arm of her chair. "You are not amusing. Do not weary our guest further than she has already been wearied by her long journey."

"Quite right," agreed Doctor Hamish. I was glad to feel his gentle touch on my back. "Come, my dear, sit by the fire," he said, guiding me towards an armchair. He glanced at Jamie, who ignored him, lunging forward for a cigarette from the box on the table and feeling in his pockets for matches.

Jamie put a cigarette in his mouth. "Smoke, Cat?"

I shrank from the offered box. What would Mother have thought? "Um … thank you, but I do not smoke."

"And nor should you," said Mrs McAllister. "Jamie, you are critical of me for pressing my opinion onto Miss Graham immediately upon her entrance, but *you* show her the discourtesy of assuming she indulges in the smoking of cigarettes! Do you not know that smoking is for girls whose mothers have abandoned their education, and who wear bloomers to ride their bicycles?"

Doctor Hamish laughed uneasily. "I am sure Catriona does not do that!"

"What if she does?" Jamie threw his head back and blew out a column of smoke. "Bloomers are an entirely practical idea."

My head ached, I was hungry and longed for my bed. I glanced at the doctor; his concern for me gave me courage. "Doctor Hamish," I began, "may I eat my supper in my room? I am so tired I can barely sit up any longer."

"Of course, I will tell Bridie. And, Jamie, will you take the trunk up, since MacGregor is not here?"

As he spoke, the arched door to the left of the fireplace opened, and Bridie, who was evidently the housekeeper, appeared with a tray bearing two bowls of broth and some bread and butter. She was about forty, thickset around the middle and not very tall, with a round face and a pinky-gold complexion, dressed in a dark blue dress and a white apron.

"Bridie," said Doctor Hamish, "our guest is very tired and will take her supper in her room."

"Aye, master, I'll take the young lady up now. I can make up another tray and bring it up the stair, no bother." She gave me a kind look. "It's a long way ye've come today, miss."

"Where's *my* soup, Bridie?" asked Jamie, on his way out of the room.

Bridie put the tray on the table. "There'll be some in the

kitchen if ye want it. Now, miss, if ye'd like to follow me."

I rose self-consciously, thanked her and turned to Jamie's grandmother. "Goodnight, Mrs McAllister. Um … I hope to hear more about, er … Scotland tomorrow."

She did not smile. "Very well, Miss Graham."

They were all looking at me. "Oh, please call me Catriona," I said.

"Then goodnight, Catriona," said Mrs McAllister, with a nod of her head.

"Goodnight, my dear," said Doctor Hamish. "Come down to breakfast as late as you like tomorrow."

I wondered how I would find the dining room. I wondered why MacGregor, who must be a manservant, was not here. I wondered, again, about Jamie's mother's whereabouts. "I am very glad to be here," I told the doctor, hoping my uncertainty did not show in my face. "Thank you for bringing me to Drumwithie. Goodnight."

The cold was noticeable as soon as Bridie and I stepped through the door into the stone-walled vestibule. "There's a good fire in your room, miss," she informed me. "If ye'd put out the lamp when ye go off to sleep that'll be fine, and just let the fire go down. I'll be up in the morning to do it."

While she spoke, I followed her up a wide stone staircase that led from the vestibule to a carpeted landing. It was no warmer up here. "It is cold all year-round, then?" I ventured.

"Aye, inside the castle. Maybe in August, after a good hot

summer, we can have a few days without fires, ye ken."

I nodded, resolving to send home for warmer underwear.

"Folk say Scotland's at its bonniest in the month of May," went on Bridie conversationally. "So ye've arrived at the right time."

As she led me along the landing I heard Jamie's boots clattering down a winding staircase in the far corner. "Trunk's at the end of the bed!" he said with an exaggerated bow. "Sleep well, bonny Cat!"

"Goodnight," I said blankly. I had not yet settled on the best way to speak to him. I did not wish to sound cold towards a young man in whose presence I was to spend the entire summer, but neither did I think it prudent to show approval of his unconventional behaviour. "Please," I added, trying to keep my tone friendly, "will you call me Catriona?"

"No, of course not!" He had already strode passed me, and was halfway along the landing. "You are *Cat* – our own mysterious Cait Sìth, is she not, Bridie? Oh! I forgot to say!" He wheeled on his heel like a soldier. "As this is your first night here, you must count the beams in your room before you sleep, and make a wish. If an unmarried girl does that, her wish will come true. Now, goodnight!"

And laughing loudly, he disappeared down the stairs.

"Och, never mind his nonsense, miss," said Bridie sympathetically. "He's full o' these tales. Mrs McAllister is fond o' telling them, so he's known them since he was a wee boy." She opened a door at the bottom of the spiral staircase, and I

42

looked inside. It was a bathroom, with a washstand, a bathtub with carved lion's feet and a water closet. "Now, if ye'd like to follow me up here to the tower."

She led me up the winding staircase, which emerged onto another, smaller landing. "Master said to put ye in the tower room, for the view."

"Oh!" A worrying thought crossed my mind. "Not the tower that's, um, in ruins?" It had not looked habitable.

Bridie was breathing noisily from our climb. "Och, no, miss!" she exclaimed, patting her chest. If she was amused at my mistake, she was too kind to show it. "The new house, as we call it, has a wee tower of its own! I'll show ye."

She opened an arched door that led off the small landing. "There's a ewer of hot water for ye in here," she said. "I ran up with the kettle and filled it as soon as I heard the pony."

I thanked her, suspecting "ran" was an exaggeration.

"Now, I'll be away to get your supper," she added.

Mother always insisted it was bad form to thank servants, but I secretly considered it impolite not to. Here at Drumwithie, I could follow my own inclination. "Thank you, Bridie," I said again.

When she had gone I turned and gazed at the room before me. It was large and oddly shaped, roughly hexagonal. The shape of the "wee tower" itself, I supposed. A log fire, covered by a guard, burned below an old-fashioned, carved mantelpiece, and there was a high bed, a chest of drawers and a closet big enough to hold a hundred times as many clothes as I had brought. The furniture stood on a Persian carpet and thick drapes hung over the windows, of which there were two, facing opposite directions.

Forgetting my weariness, I ran to the nearest window and pushed back the curtain. All was blackness. But as I stood there, gooseflesh crept over my arms. I was certain that, like an eagle in its eyrie, whoever gazed from this window had command of Drumwithie estate and all that lay beyond it to the horizon. A magnificent aspect awaited me in the morning.

Bridie's footsteps sounded on the stairs, and she appeared with my soup, the bowl covered by a tin lid. She put the tray on the table and retreated a few steps. "Ye'll remember to turn out the lamp, will ye not, miss?"

"I promise."

"Well, if there's nothing else ye want, I'll be away down the stair."

"Thank you. Goodnight."

"Goodnight, miss."

And with that, she left me alone. Nervously, I looked up at the ceiling. There were four beams, but I did not know what to wish for. It was certainly an odd superstition. And why had Jamie said I was their mysterious Cait Sìth? Cait perhaps meant cat, but Sìth?

Shrugging, I sat down at the table and took the lid off the bowl of soup. I felt the steam on my face, picked up the spoon and began to eat ravenously, as if I had not had a morsel for days. The broth was delicious, and Bridie had also brought the end of a fresh loaf and a dish of butter. I ate happily for a few minutes, but when I picked up the knife to spread the butter on the bread I heard a sound. It was such an odd sound I paused, the knife in my hand, straining my ears. There it was again: a sound somewhere between loud and soft, between inside and outside the house, between a human voice and an animal cry.

I put down the knife. It clinked against the plate and I jumped. "Silly girl!" I scolded myself aloud. There was nothing to be nervous of. And yet I *was* nervous. I began again on my soup, but before I had swallowed the first mouthful, I heard the sound again.

I stood up. Something or someone was speaking, or weeping, or moaning. Something was in this tower with me. Nervousness turned to fear. My heart felt heavy, dragged down by the weight of the blood pumping through it, and I put my hand over it, feeling it pulsing under my blouse. *Nobody's heart throbs like that unless there is something to be frightened of,* I reasoned. My body was telling me to be wary.

I went first to one wall, then another in the strangely shaped room, listening closely at each. I opened the huge cupboard, which contained only spare pillows and blankets. I flung back the curtains at both windows. Nothing but darkness. And yet the sound went on. I closed my eyes, listening intently, trying to identify what it could possibly be.

The wind? There had been none when we drove up to

45

the castle. Cautiously, I opened one of the windows a few inches, and put my hand out. The air was still.

Someone crying? A child? But there were no children in the house.

A woman keening sorrowfully, like a mourner by a graveside? That was the nearest approximation I could make. I pushed the casement farther open and leaned over the sill. Light from the downstairs rooms made yellow patches on the gravel path, but revealed nothing. No woman, no child, no grave.

I was certain I was not imagining it. I could still hear it after I closed the window, louder than when it was open. The sounds were *here* in this room, and whatever was making them was here too.

"Come out and show me who you are!" I demanded. My voice sounded shrill and filled with panic. I knew I would not sleep until I had confronted whatever it was that had so disturbed my peace. I listened for a moment; the sound diminished in intensity, but grew again, bitter and harrowing, when I moved towards the table. I put my hands over my ears, but could not obliterate it.

Then suddenly, it diminished to silence. I took my hands from my ears. As I did so I saw something so unexpected I had to clamp my teeth together to prevent myself from shrieking. I gazed in silence as a woman approached me from the direction of the window. No, not a woman, a young girl of about my age. Stiff with astonishment, I lunged for the knife on the table and gripped the handle. Where had she come from? No one had followed me and the door had not opened.

I could neither speak nor scream. My heart pounded, blood sang in my ears, but I could not move. The young woman stepped noiselessly nearer. Her pale skin looked as delicate as a child's. Tangled, dark hair hung over her shoulders, and her dress was of the fashion popular twenty years ago, with an apron-style front gathered to a bustle at the back, and a low, tight bodice. The dress was creased, and even torn in places, as if she had been wearing it for a long time without an opportunity to tidy herself. The colour had once been pink, the material silk, but so much filth clung to it, especially around the hem, I could only guess how beautiful it might once have been.

I looked into the face that sought mine. She had oval-shaped eyes, dark like my own. But their expression was unlike anything I had ever seen. She gazed at me with a suffering so elemental it chilled me to my bones. And then, although I did not turn away, or even blink, I no longer saw her. She simply vanished.

I gasped aloud with fear. This was surely the woman whose screams I had heard. She must be an apparition, something unreal. My schoolfriends had told ghost stories, which were enjoyably frightening because they were exactly that: stories. But this was *real*.

Trembling, I sat at the table again, put down the knife and

tried to calm myself. Count the beams, Jamie had said, and your wishes will come true. I looked up and counted one, two, three, four beams, wishing fervently that what I had just experienced was the product of fatigue and overwrought nerves.

Counting the beams soothed my fear. But I did not pick up the spoon to finish the now-cold soup. I stumbled to the bed and lay down on it fully dressed, waiting tensely for the sound to return. When it did not, relief rushed over me with such force I was too numb to move. And without removing my boots or turning down the lamp, I tumbled into sleep.

1893

Seventeen years previously

*I*n her dream, the bare, sun-warmed rock felt smooth on her back, like the touch of another person's skin. She lay there, looking at the sky, filled with loneliness and longing and love. He had risen from beside her, put on his shirt and stepped down from the outcrop without a word. If she sat up, she would see him making his way across the glen. She would watch him enter the shadow of the wood, the sun alighting for the last time upon his golden hair.

But she did not sit up. She could not bear to prolong the parting, to cling feebly to a final view of him. She was stronger than that; she would lie here until she was calm, and her cheeks were pale again, and then she would return to the house. She would take her place at one end of the table, her husband at the other, and they would speak briefly of their visitor's departure. Her husband might express his hope that the train was punctual and his cousin's journey pleasant. She would push her food around her plate, and think of his bright hair, the sensation of his fingers upon her flesh, and the wound his departure had left in her heart.

And then she was screaming. On and on she screamed, pouring her despair into the empty valley and the bare rock under the sky.

"Mama! Mama!"

The child's cry entered her hearing, but she did not understand where it had come from. Then she felt his small hand touch hers, and his knees dig into her thigh as he climbed onto the sofa beside her. "Mama, you are crying!"

She sat up, coughing, and caught him in her arms. She stroked the white-gold hair she could not bear to cut, even though the boy had passed his fourth birthday. "Mama is well, darling," she reassured him. "I was dreaming, that is all."

He gazed up at her, his cheeks streaked with tears. "Not-nice dream," he said gravely.

"You are quite right," she said, embracing him once more. "It was one of Mama's not-nice dreams. Now, will you let me rest a little longer? Bridie will take care of you."

IT HAS BEGUN

J amie was sitting on the window seat, reading a book. I hesitated in the doorway, having opened a door at random with no idea that it led to the library. "Oh, I'm sorry. I'm disturbing you."

I began to shut the door, but he closed his book with a loud thud. "Stay there!"

"Aren't you reading?"

"Who would want to read, when he could indulge in conversation with a beautiful cat?" He approached me, leaving his book on the window seat. His uncombed hair covered one eye, and he was wearing an extraordinary mixture of garments: yellowish linen trousers, a loose shirt and a waistcoat embroidered with serpents and flowers in the Chinese style. His feet were bare. "Did you sleep well? Cats usually do."

"Jamie…" I gathered my courage. "May I ask you again to call me Catriona? I do not understand why you have named me 'Cat'."

"Then I must tell you about the Cait Sìth." He plumped down in an armchair, put his feet on the fender and pointed to the other armchair. "Sit there and you will hear all. Oh, and did you count the beams?"

I had not yet decided whether to tell him what had happened last night. "No," I said coolly.

"Ach!" He clapped his hand to his head. "And now you've missed your chance! You have to do it only on the *first night* you spend in a place or it doesn't work. Now we will have to change your bedroom!"

I sat down. "Jamie, you will not have to change my bedroom. It is a *story*, a superstition. Bridie says you have got these stories from your grandmother. Is that true?"

"Quite true. My family adores superstitions!" He swept his arm round theatrically. "See all these books? Collected by my grandfather Buchanan, who had a great interest in Scottish myths and legends."

"And did your grandfather Buchanan believe in them?"

He gazed at me, green eyes alert for mockery. "No. His interest was scholarly. But I sometimes think my grandmother believes them."

"Because it is she who likes to tell the stories?"

He nodded, his eyes remaining on my face. "She is absolutely unshakeable in her belief that Scottish legends and folklore must be preserved. Before you have been here one more day, she will corner you and lecture you about the committee she sits on in Edinburgh, and how important its work is." He smiled suddenly, transforming his face into that of a delighted child. "And you will be too polite to escape! I wish you luck, bonny Cat!"

I sighed. "You were about to tell me about a legend yourself, were you not? What is this Cait Sìth? Something to do with a cat, by any chance?"

He swung his feet off the fender and sat forward eagerly. "A cat, yes, but a special cat. A faerie cat."

I almost laughed. "A *fairy* cat?"

"Not an English fairy such as you are envisaging," he said, no longer smiling. "The faerie folk are not tiny, winged things who live at the bottom of the garden. They are … a presence. The Gaelic word for them is the *sìth*." He was looking intently into my face. "They do things that would otherwise be unexplained, and they appear in various forms. The Cait Sìth, which means 'Faerie Cat', is a large black cat, too large to be a domestic cat, encountered all over Scotland on heaths and moors and mountains. No one has ever caught it, or photographed it, so its existence has passed into legend. In people's minds, you see, if it isn't a real cat, it must be a supernatural one, sent by the faerie folk."

"Do they really call them that?" I asked doubtfully. "The faerie folk?"

"In Scots, yes. The word is spelled f-a-e-r-i-e."

"It sounds most unlikely."

"It is only unlikely, my dear English girl, to those who have the luxury of education and scepticism. Scotland is a harsh place for poor people, cold and mountainous. Daily survival is governed by the landscape, the tides, the weather, animals, fish, birds – did you know that on some islands the inhabitants actually eat seabirds? So it isn't surprising that superstitions grow up about unexplained things."

I said nothing. Despite my scepticism, which he had pointed out, and my impatience with his "Cat" joke, which I had pointed out, I was interested.

"You are like a cat, you see," he said unexpectedly. "You are dark like the Cait Sìth, and your brow is smooth and pale like the white patch it has on its face. Your eyes are as black as your hair, and with every look they say to the world, *I am clever, I am disdainful, I am myself.*" He leaned nearer me, apparently unaware of my pink cheeks. "The Cait Sìth is mysterious, an interloper, an unknown. It is magnificent to look at, but if approached, it will attack. It has determination, and strength. And yet it blends into its surroundings so well that no one would notice it, unless they were looking for it."

I was not sure if it was Jamie's intention to flatter me. My experience of young men was limited. The few boys of my own age I had been introduced to, usually sons of my parents' acquaintances, or brothers of schoolfriends, had been more interested in beating me at tennis than flirting with me. I resented Jamie's words – what right did they have to cause such an unbecoming flush? – and yet his seriousness and eloquence had touched me, and I could not voice my resentment.

"Do you really think these things apply to *me*?" I asked instead.

He sat back and contemplated me solemnly. "Yes, indeed. It is the faerie folk who have sent you, and your supernatural ways, to our little household here at Drumwithie."

I digested this, my thoughts racing again to the tower room. Perhaps the cries I had heard were from a supernatural source – something ghostly, like the Cait Sìth, spoken of but not seen. But I was not yet ready to surrender to this notion. It still sounded preposterous.

"Really?" I said drily. "I was under the impression that it was your father who brought me to Drumwithie."

"He did," he agreed, still watching my face. "But I must tell you, when he read the notice in *The Times* that morning, there was a look on his face I'd never seen before. It was as if he had been released from a heavy burden."

My interest increased, and I sat forward. "What did he say?"

"He told us his cousin, David Graham, had died, and he felt bound to pay his respects despite a long estrangement. He wrote to the funeral director and went down south for the funeral. Then we received a telegram telling us he would be bringing David Graham's daughter back with him to spend the summer at Drumwithie. After she had read it, Grandmother said, 'Hamish's intention in bringing this young woman here is clear. The time has come for him to heal a deep wound.'"

I remembered Doctor Hamish's words to my mother about the estrangement: *it concerned a personal matter which he would not wish me to disclose, even now.* "Jamie," I began carefully, "do you know what happened between our fathers, to cause this wound your grandmother spoke of?"

He shrugged, fixing me with a calm gaze. "I am as much in the dark as you. But whatever it was, it meant I grew up never hearing of Miss Catriona Graham, and you grew up never hearing of Mr James Buchanan."

I willed myself to go on looking at him, though another flush threatened. "Your grandmother is correct," I told him. "Your father is trying to heal a wound, in bringing me to a place my father was once fond of, but was banished from for many years. Also, he very kindly seeks to give me a holiday, after the many months of illness and now the, um, passing of my father, which is like a cloud Mother and I have been living under. If she had not had so much to deal with at our factory, he would have brought her too."

Jamie nodded, unable to argue with this.

"And there is one more thing he said," I continued before I lost courage. "He told us you consider Drumwithie a little restricted and would enjoy having some company for the summer."

"Ah!" He smiled with a sort of relieved satisfaction. "Of *course*. To entertain me during my last summer at home, I suppose he said?"

"He said you are to enter the Medical School at Edinburgh in the autumn."

"Hm." His face straightened, and he stared moodily at the floor. His forelock had fallen over his eyes; I could not interpret his expression. He took a deep breath, as if nerve were needed to speak his next words. "The only person who thinks I am ever going to be a doctor is my father." He looked up at me through the curtain of golden hair. "You see, Cat, I am a poet."

The thought of Jamie as a poet made me smile, though I should have suspected such a thing. Unkempt hair, strange attire and stranger behaviour were the hallmarks of a romantic.

"Of course you are a poet!" I said delightedly. "Will you show me your work?"

"No. At least, not yet. I am not satisfied with any of it, and I will not allow you, *especially* you, to read second-rate rubbish."

"Then tell me what you are reading," I said, glancing at the book he had left on the window seat. "If I am to be your company for the whole summer I had better find out if we have any interests in common. Though personally, I doubt it."

"There you are, you see!" He leapt out of his chair – did he ever move carefully or slowly?

His face was alive again, smiling, his hair bouncing as he lunged for the book. "The cat sits there as quiet as you like, then out of the blue, it bares its claws!"

He tossed the book onto the table. It was a book of poetry. I picked it up and read the title aloud. "*Poems*, by W. B. Yeats."

"It's pronounced 'Yates'," said Jamie, impatiently enough for me to feel my ignorance. "He's Irish. A wonderful, mystical poet."

I could not resist. "You mean, he writes about f-a-e-r-i-e folk and so on?"

"I suppose so," sighed Jamie. "But if you actually *read* it, you will see that it is sublime."

I put the book down unopened. "I am sure it is. And one day, so will your poetry be."

"Do not patronize me, Cat."

The library was utterly silent. It was a large, square room with a prominent window at the front of the house. It did not overlook the courtyard where the kitchen and stables were, and Drumwithie's thick walls prevented any sounds made by the servants from reaching us. At breakfast Doctor Hamish had told me he was going to his surgery in Drumwithie, on the back, I supposed, of a younger horse than Kelpie. Jamie had apparently already finished breakfast and Mrs McAllister had not appeared at all.

A log on the fire shifted, throwing out sparks. I could not think what to say; there seemed no sensible observation to make. Doctor Hamish's hesitation when the subject of Jamie came up, the examinations that had required "a few attempts", my mother's cross comment about getting there in the end – I remembered it all very clearly. And now the cause of the frostiness between Jamie and his father was clear.

"My father seems to think that just because he is interested in medicine, then everyone must be," he told me testily. "But I do not expect everyone to be a poet, merely because I am one, do I?"

"No, indeed," I replied obediently.

"He cannot understand that poetry is just as important as healing sick people and delivering babies and all those things he does," continued Jamie. He began to stride restlessly about the room, becoming more agitated as he spoke. "Art can heal, and inspire, and be a godly thing, as much as anything a doctor does, can it not? But he thinks the only thing in the world is science, science, science! He only respects people if they are scientists, or are in some other equally dull field such as the law, or the management of money, or the construction of buildings. He hangs on the every word of those quacks that treat my poor mother. But they *are* quacks, Cat, every one! My mother's condition is pitiable, to be sure, but it is incurable, and I wish my father would admit it!"

I swallowed, trying to take in what he had said. But before I could reply, he threw himself down in the chair again and kicked the table. "Sometimes I hate him," he said bitterly. "I absolutely *hate* him!"

My father's love for me, and mine for him, was an immoveable truth that had supported me all my life. I could not imagine hating a father, let alone voicing my hatred to a virtual stranger. I was shocked, but Jamie's frustration had also stirred my heart. I did not disapprove of his admission; I was sorry for it. "I believe," I said guardedly, "your father is a good man."

"Hmph!"

"Jamie, I do not think—"

He was not listening. "Do you know about my mother? What has he told you?"

I tried to remember Doctor Hamish's words about his wife. "I believe he told us she is away at present. He did not mention that she was ill."

Jamie gave an exaggerated sigh. "Well, she is. She lives in a hospital, and has done these last seven years. She always suffered from nerves, and I remember her having terrible nightmares. When I was a small boy she had some sort of collapse, and different doctors came to see her, and of course none of them could do anything. Then, when they finally took her to the hospital..." He sighed again. "Well, they tried to keep it from me, but I was fourteen then, and my grandmother knew I was old enough to hear the truth. She told me that they had taken my mother away because she tried to kill herself."

I felt cold. The sound of a woman in distress. Cries of unbearable sorrow. I stared at him. "You are sure that your mother is in a hospital, are you not?" I asked.

Understandably, he was nonplussed at such an odd question. He stared back at me, his eyes dulled by incomprehension. "What in God's name do you mean? Of course I am sure. How could I be mistaken about such a thing?"

"I'm sorry," I said hurriedly. "But ... have you read a book called *Jane Eyre*?"

"No. I have heard of it, though. It is so famous, I should think everyone has."

"In it there is a woman whom they pretend is dead," I told him, "but really she is locked in an attic. She cries in the night, and the heroine, Jane Eyre, hears her, and wonders what the sound is."

Jamie rolled his eyes. "That sounds like the plot of every ghastly gothic novel my grandmother has ever left strewn about the place. Do you honestly read such rubbish?"

"*Jane Eyre* is not rubbish!" I leapt to defend the book that had made such a profound impression on me. "It is not a ghastly gothic novel. It is more ... a romance. Anyway, the point is, my room is in the attic here – well, the tower. And something happened there last night."

I hesitated while his contemptuous stare turned to one of interest.

"I heard something," I told him. Now the confession was made, I felt less foolish than I had feared. "It was the sound of a woman crying, or more like shrieking, in desperation or agony. It was so loud! I looked out of the window, thinking it was the wind. I even opened the cupboard. But there was nothing. And when you told me about your mother, I just thought—"

"She is in a hospital in Edinburgh, I tell you!" he protested. "She has not been at Drumwithie these seven years, more's the pity!"

"Very well. But when I tell you what happened next, perhaps you will be able to offer an explanation."

Jamie was as still as a stone, his face a picture of bewilderment. I paused, uncertain how to explain, afraid he would laugh. In daylight, here in the comfort of the library, I was no longer sure that my senses could be trusted. "Before I go on," I said at last, "will you promise me that you will not think I am the sort of girl who makes up stories to get attention, or considers herself 'sensitive'?"

His face relaxed, though he did not smile. "Of course. It is obvious you aren't."

"Very well, then. When the sound began to fade way, I saw what I must describe as a ghost. It was certainly not a real person, though it was in the form of a young girl. She appeared from nowhere, not through the door or a window. I was so frightened, I thought I would faint."

"Good God!" Jamie's expression had changed. He stood up, blinking rapidly, very agitated. "Are you sure you did not fall asleep and—"

"I am sure. She stood there as plainly as you are standing now."

"You are *sure*?"

"I have just said I am."

"And what did she do, this ghost? Did she speak?"

"No, she did not speak. She looked at me and I at her. Her face was full of such sorrow, I cannot describe it. It affected me greatly. I pitied her."

"What did she look like? Her colouring, I mean? Was she fair?"

"No, dark. And she wore a pink dress, very dirty." As I described her, I remembered more and more. "An old-fashioned dress, from twenty or more years ago."

His eyes, fixed on my face, looked glassy. "And she was young, you say?"

"Yes, a girl about my age."

"And she did not speak or cry out?"

Agitation was making him repeat himself. "Jamie, I have told you she did not."

"But the woman's voice you heard before she appeared – it could have been hers, could it not?"

"I assumed it was."

"But it might not have been. It might have been something, or someone else, entirely."

I was confused. "I suppose so, but why?"

"Why should anything be what it seems?" He was fumbling in his pocket for his cigarettes. "This is not the natural world, dearest Cat, but the supernatural one. If you really did see this young girl in her old-fashioned dress, then she was visiting you from the Other Side, where she has been since her death." He paused while he lit a cigarette and took his first pull on it. His hand shook a little. "And it came to *you*. You may not believe you are associated with the Other World, but that ghost, that spirit, certainly does!"

I stared at him. "Do you mean she is communicating through *me*?"

"Why not? She has visited you. You alone saw her, and

heard the voice, because you are the Cait Sìth." He sucked on the cigarette again, his cheeks hollowing, and blew out the smoke around his head. "This spirit has returned, after all this time. The dress was from twenty years ago, you say? Because you have come, she can reveal herself."

He sat down again, still agitated, smoking hurriedly, his shoulders hunched. Without knowing what I was doing, I fell to my knees on the hearthrug. "So you think I have some sort of *gift*?" I asked guardedly.

"Inasmuch as I believe in the spiritual world," he replied, "I believe you are the channel through which she is speaking to us."

"But you are not sure you *do* believe in the spiritual world?"

He narrowed his eyes. "Yesterday, I was unsure. Today, I am *more* sure. Tomorrow, if this visitor comes again, I will be *absolutely* sure."

As I knelt there, my hands in my lap, my hair coming loose as usual, I felt that a revelation had been made to me. I felt freed from some nameless imprisonment. I felt clear-headed and forward-looking. "I am already sure," I told him. "And I am also sure that this young woman has some connection with the tower bedroom. Maybe she died here. Do you know of any such thing?"

He leaned forward to throw his cigarette butt into the fire, his face troubled. "No, though of course people must have been dying at Drumwithie for hundreds of years. But the girl's dress from twenty years ago... I confess myself to be as baffled as you are."

We pondered in silence for a moment. I gazed into the fire; Jamie rested his head on the cushion and looked at the ceiling. "You *did* count the beams in the tower room, didn't you?" he said unexpectedly.

"Yes, I did. There are four." I decided to be cautious. "But I did not know what to wish for, so the charm probably did not work."

He smiled; he knew I was telling him less than the truth, but he did not pursue it. "Perhaps the Cait Sìth needs no charms to work its magic."

I got to my feet and stood before the fire. It warmed my legs through my thin dress, and lit Jamie's features unevenly. "Even if it did work," I pointed out, "it would scarcely help me understand what is happening."

"I do not understand it either." His eyes met mine straight on. They looked very green. "But it is certainly magic."

He was silent for a long time. No birds sang outside; the only sound in the room was a faint crackling from the log fire. I went on standing there before the fire, and he went on sitting in the chair, and then he spoke again. "And I feel sure the magic will soon become clear. The winding of the spell has already begun. Because you have come to Drumwithie, it has begun."

OPHELIA

S uddenly Jamie stood up, lunged forward and grasped my hand. "Come on, there's something I wish to show you!"

He led me through the Great Hall to the door on the right-hand side of the fireplace. Beyond it was a flight of stone stairs leading downwards, so ancient that a hollow had been worn in the centre of each tread. At the bottom of the stairs was another stone-floored passage, wider than the one that led to the library. It was so dark I could hardly see my feet. Jamie's fingers enclosed mine very tightly.

The passage ended in an arched door studded with nails. Jamie lifted the iron latch, and we entered a small room where scarves and hats hung on hooks, and several pairs of boots lay on their sides to dry off after cleaning. Plainly, we were at the back entrance of the house, in the boot room.

"MacGregor has been busy this morning, as you see," said Jamie. He dropped my hand; he needed both of his to put his boots on. "If there's one thing he can't stand, it's a neglected pair of boots. If you leave your dirty ones here, they'll be immaculate by the next time you need them."

"Is MacGregor your butler?" I took the opportunity to ask.

"Butler?" repeated Jamie, looking up from his boots with more incredulity than my question deserved. "No! There has never been a butler at Drumwithie in my lifetime. Bridie does everything indoors."

"Then who is he?"

"He is the gillie."

I was none the wiser. "The gillie?"

He straightened up and went to the enormous oak door in the outside wall. The bolt was so large it took both his hands, and some strength, to shift it. "He likes to say his job is three 'gs' – groom, gardener and gillie. That is, what you would call a gamekeeper."

The day was sunny, but a breeze blew Jamie's hair this way and that as we stepped outside. "If MacGregor had been here last night," he went on, "he would have driven you and Father from the station and taken your box up to your room, but he was down in Drumwithie, getting drunk, as he does every Saturday night. Saturday is his half-day off. I never mind driving the trap on a Saturday if it is needed. Indeed, I enjoy it. Have you not got such a man at home?"

"Well … not really. The estate at Chester House is farm-land, so the game is managed by the tenant farmer. My father was never fond of shooting anyway." I shaded my eyes with my hand. "But we do have a butler. His name is Jarvis. And we have a gardener and a groom. It must be hard work for MacGregor to do all those jobs himself."

Jamie stopped so unexpectedly, I almost walked into him. He was grinning like a madman, his face transformed, not into a delighted child this time, but into a clown. Without a word, he positioned his arms above his head in a graceful arc and began to dance a Highland fling. He looked so ridiculous, jigging in his yellow trousers and Chinese waistcoat, with his hair bouncing and his booted feet pointing, I burst into laughter. Then I laughed more as he began to sing, in broad Scots, to a well-known Scottish tune:

> *"Och a Scotsmon can dae three-ee times*
> *The wurrk of ony Englishmon.*
> *He gruims, he garrdens, guarrds the deerr.*
> *He puits all comerrs un theirr place,*
> *And is hame in time for hus beerr, ho!"*

I was laughing so much my ribs were beginning to ache. "Stop!" I begged breathlessly.

He obeyed me, dropping his hands to his hips. His face was serious again. "You look wonderful, Cat," he said.

The untidy outline of his head was blurred; laughter had made my eyes water. Why did he say I looked wonderful? He had used the same word about Yeats's poetry. Mystical, wonderful, sublime. I knew I was none of those things: I

68

was wearing last year's grey summer dress with a black ribbon round my throat, my usual woollen stockings and black boots. I was not, as Mother would put it, "got up smart".

And if my clothes did not look wonderful, neither did my hair. Attacked by the same breeze that had tangled Jamie's, it had come loose and flapped in curtains around my cheeks. It was straighter than I liked, and I had to curl it with papers when I wished to look nice, but last night I had fallen asleep without putting them in. I was certain I looked untidy; the mirror in the hallway at Chester House had often shown me exactly what my hair looked like on my return from a walk, on days less windy than this.

Furthermore, I realized to my embarrassment, I had violated the first rule of acceptable behaviour for a lady, especially one in mourning: I had gone outside without a hat.

"I do *not* look wonderful," I said, putting up my hand to tidy my hair. It was unsuccessful; the wind blew it over my face again as soon as I took my hand away. "You pulled me out of the house so quickly, I did not even put on my hat."

"Exactly. You look wonderfully *wild*."

I straightened my shoulders. "I thought you brought me out here to show me something. It will be time for luncheon before we have taken two more steps."

He put his head on one side. "My dear Cat, do you not recognize a compliment when you hear it?"

"Of course I do," I told him. "But, please, do not say such

things. They make me uncomfortable."

"Very well. But *I* shall not be uncomfortable should you wish to give *me* a compliment. I absolutely adore compliments!"

I did not return his smile. After a moment he resumed walking, forwards this time, until he turned abruptly right, between two hedges. "This is Anne's Garden, as we call it," he announced. "It was made by my mother when she was first married, and she always tended it. I used to help her sometimes when I was small. MacGregor does it now, of course."

I followed him down some steps to a pretty hollow, carpeted with grass and criss-crossed with paths. Alpine plants tumbled over a rockery, and wrought-iron tables and chairs had been placed to take full advantage of the panorama. I went to the waist-high wall at the garden's edge and gazed at the view. A haze hung in the late morning air; the horizon shimmered. From the pines that covered the mountainside rose a scent like no other – medicinal, sweet, harsh yet pleasant. The scent of Drumwithie.

I looked back at the house. One of my bedroom windows overlooked the hillside we had driven up last night and the other the wooded glen. This garden was at the side of the castle, above a sheer drop from the rock on which Drumwithie sat. It was a dramatic place and a disturbing sight. I wondered whether, given the choice, I would have made a garden in a position with a more tranquil aspect.

"Over here is the well," said Jamie.

I followed him past the rockery and round the corner, our backs to the view. Between patches of thinning grass, the soles of my boots encountered ancient cobblestones.

"This well is our only source of fresh water," Jamie told me. It was an ordinary-looking well, a hole in the ground surrounded by a low stone wall. Unsure what he expected me to say, I remained silent. "The spring rises in the caves beneath where we are standing," he continued. "There is a pool down there that feeds the well."

He put one knee on the wall, leaned over and gazed into the water. This cobbled space was sheltered from the wind and shaded by pines. His green eyes looked darker in this light, almost the colour of the trees themselves.

"Shall we go back now?" I asked.

"But I haven't shown you the caves yet!"

I frowned, confused. His tendency to spin his mood on a sixpence was unnerving. "What caves?"

He took off at a fast pace, back towards the boot room. "Need a lantern!" When he emerged he was holding a glass-sided carriage lamp. "The caves in the rock, under the castle," he explained. "In ancient times people lived in them and Grandmother told me they were used for storage until about a hundred years ago. They are particularly well-preserved, my father says." He lit the lantern and blew out the match. "'The finest caves in Christendom, Jamie!' I can hear him now, the pompous oaf."

"Do not speak of him like that!" I had encountered several

71

pompous oafs among my parents' acquaintances, but Doctor Hamish was not one of them.

"I will speak of him however I wish. Now, follow me and mind your step. I would not like to have to carry you home on my shoulder."

The entrance to the caves was low and almost hidden by undergrowth. Jamie crouched and pushed it aside. "Go on," he urged. "It's quite safe."

I stepped into a narrow space with a flat stone floor. When Jamie held the lantern up, it showed the slime-covered rock of the ceiling. "Ugh!" I exclaimed. "How damp it is in here!"

"It gets drier as you go on. I want you to see my favourite cave."

A smaller cave led off the first one, and from that, a staircase hewn from the stone. "Up here," said Jamie. His voice echoed in the gloom. I wished we had stayed in the garden; I instinctively shrank from these caves, "fine" or not. Above were trees and sky; here there was only rock, and damp, and impenetrable darkness.

I followed Jamie through a labyrinth of passages, some smoothed by human hands, others so rough and low we had to stoop almost double. Several times I stumbled on loose stones, but Jamie hauled me to my feet without a word and we continued.

His favourite cave had what might be called a window – a narrow slit where two boulders met. Someone had hollowed out a primitive seat beside it. "I used to come here a lot when

I was a boy," he said. "And I still come sometimes to get away from Father and to think about Mother." He breathed deeply in, and out again. "It was down here that she was found. She tried to drown herself in the pool that feeds the well. If MacGregor had not noticed trampling of the plants at the entrance, she would have succeeded."

I could not think what to say. Into my head came the memory of a painting that had hung on the Art Room wall at St Giles's College. It was a reproduction of a famous work by Sir John Everett Millais, depicting Ophelia, the girl in Shakespeare's tragedy *Hamlet*, lying in the stream where she had drowned herself. Miss Gunter, the art mistress, had talked a lot about the brush technique and the school of artists Millais belonged to, and medieval influences on British painting of the last century. But all I had thought about was poor Ophelia, with her thin gown floating on the water, her rippled hair decked with flowers. She looked as if she were lying on a bier. In my schoolgirl's imagination she was not a fictional character, but a real girl like me. How could someone so young have been driven to such an act?

There was a sudden shriek. I started violently, unconsciously grabbing Jamie's arm. "What was that?"

"A hawk, I should think."

"Oh!" The caves were making me nervous. How could Jamie bear to come down to the place where his mother had almost died? "Er ... are there any more caves or is this the last one?"

"No, there are more." He held the lantern so that we could see each other's faces. "This glen is ancient landscape, carved out of the rock in the Ice Age. It probably contains more caves than have yet been discovered. The reason Father thinks our caves are so fine is their geological significance, which, being a scientist, he is very proud of. But I am more interested in their history. How did ancient people, without modern tools, hew the stone? They had water, from the spring, but how did they cook their food and keep warm? There is nowhere for smoke to escape."

I listened, but I could not pretend I shared his interest. I was beginning to be overtaken by loathing of the place. "Shall we go back up now?" I asked.

"You used to be able to get into another cave," he went on, ignoring my request, leading the way yet further into the darkness, "from the side of the glen. But the entrance has been blocked for years. Sometimes the land shifts and trees fall."

"Oh, yes! I noticed that."

From my window in the tower I had seen the huge trees that grew out of the glenside, twisted with age, some almost horizontal, their roots clinging to the mossy earth, apparently defying gravity. Some had fallen, and their carcasses lay at the bottom of the glen, tossed there like bodies in a paupers' grave.

"Shall we go and see the pool?" suggested Jamie.

"Um … thank you, but I don't think I want to."

He stared at me. "Why not?"

74

"Well, if it is the place… I mean, I do not understand why you want to take me there, or go there yourself."

He went on staring. "So will you never visit your father's grave?"

"Jamie, please…" I did not know what he meant. His mother was not dead.

"Does it not occur to you," he said, tight-lipped, "that this is the last place on earth that witnessed my mother as she was, before her mind disintegrated completely? The day she came down here and entered the pool, she had spoken to me at breakfast about geography. A map I had drawn had impressed her. Everyone else was out. I was at my books, doing Latin verbs in the library. It was an ordinary Wednesday. And then it wasn't. It was the worst Wednesday of our lives. Now, shall we go and see the pool?"

I could have given way and followed him meekly. But I did not. His story had horrified me − the thought that this woman, the wife of a respected doctor and the mother of a fourteen-year-old boy, could descend to this dark place and slip, like Ophelia, into the freezing water, made me shudder. So I did what Jamie himself had admired me for: I bared my claws.

"No," I told him firmly. "I do not wish to look at the pool, ever. In fact, I never want to come down to these horrible caves again."

I thought he would sigh, turn and lead the way back up into the sunshine. But he did not. He committed what I thought must be an act of madness. He hurled the lantern against the wall of the cave, smashing the glass and extinguishing the light. I heard it clatter to the floor, but I could see almost nothing. The only light now was the greyish glow from the slit between the boulders. "What are you doing?" I screamed. "How will we find our way back ?"

"*I* can find my way back perfectly easily," came his voice, now farther away. "You, though, who consider the caves *horrible*, and won't go and see the pool where my mother tried to *die*, can stay here for ever, for all I care."

His tone was perfectly measured; he was not agitated in any way. I stumbled in the direction of his voice, but the farther I went from the window-slit, the less light there was. And then I realized he was not there. He had gone back down one of the passages and was making his way out, along a route he knew so well he could follow it in the dark.

Panic gripped me. "Jamie!" I screamed. "Come back! I will go with you to the pool!"

Silence. But not quite silence. A faint *swoosh*, like the hem of a woman's gown brushing a carpet, came to my ears. I put my hand over my mouth to stop myself from screaming again, and strained my ears. Any noise, however small, must come from the entrance to the cave, so I must follow it.

Nothing happened for a moment. Then I heard the sound again. It was followed almost instantaneously by another sound: the *plink-plink* of dripping water. Relief rushed through me. I must be standing near the water at the bottom of the well. The pool I had refused to visit must be farther away, and water from it was intermittently falling over stone – *swoosh* – and splashing into the well water – *plink-plink*. Hoping that, since the well was open to the sky, enough light would filter down to allow me to see my surroundings, I groped my way along the wall in the direction of the sounds.

I was right; the wall of the cave ended abruptly, and I came upon the well. The surface of the water was disturbed now and then by the influx of fresh water from the pool, which in turn was fed by the spring. *Plink-plink, bubble-bubble.* Comforted by the sound, I craned my neck to look up the stone-lined shaft to the round hole at the top, from where Jamie had gazed down at this very water. I was not so far from civilization, I told myself. I had no intention whatsoever of making my way back through the pitch-blackness of the caves, but if Jamie did not come back, and I could not make anyone hear my cries for help, I could climb up the iron ladder bolted to the side of the well.

I called up the shaft. All I heard was the echo of my own voice, then the silence again descended. I waited for a few moments, in case Jamie came back. But my fear was increasing. I had to get out.

I piled my skirt and petticoats untidily into the waistband of my drawers. It was fortuitous, after all, that I was not "got up smart". Trying not to look into the black depths, I reached for the iron ladder and gave it a tug. It was secure. I stood on the first rung. It held my weight. I muttered words of encouragement to myself, trying to blot from my memory the moment when Jamie had smashed the lantern. Then I lifted my face towards the circle of daylight and began to climb.

PART TWO

THE
CHANGELING

A LEGEND AS OLD
AS TIME

"Good grief, Catriona, what has happened to you?"

It was Mrs McAllister's voice – Scottish, but without the softness of Bridie's. Rather shrill, in fact. She was striding up the gravel path, her skirt held clear of a pair of stout boots, wearing a feather-trimmed hat and a determined look. Beside her was a kilted man, with a shapeless tam-o'-shanter on his head and a stick in his hand. His sturdy legs were encased in thick socks, and under his tweed coat he wore a woollen pullover. It might be a fine day in May, but he was dressed for an outdoors wilder than the castle gardens. His face was neither old nor young, reddish, with whiskers round the chin and a large nose. This must be MacGregor, the gillie.

Mrs McAllister stopped in front of me, trying to shield my unconventional appearance from MacGregor. He hung back and had the tact to examine the horizon while she looked me up and down incredulously. "Where in heaven's name have you been, to make yourself so dirty?"

Clearly, she had not seen me emerge from the well. I wondered if the gillie had. "Jamie was showing me the caves under the castle," I explained, pulling my skirts free of my drawers and shaking them out. "So I saved my dress by tucking it in."

"In front of *my grandson*?" she asked, horrified. "What were you thinking, child? What would your mother think?"

"Jamie had gone by then," I said lamely. Her expression demanded an explanation, so I pressed on. "He had to go somewhere, he didn't say where, so I found my own way out." I looked down at my dirt-smeared bodice. "It is damp down there. I must have brushed against a wall."

She drew herself up and studied me disapprovingly. "Hm. Well, MacGregor," she said, half-turning to him, "this is Miss Graham."

He touched his hat. "Good day to ye, miss."

I scarcely had time to nod before Mrs McAllister addressed him again. "MacGregor, we really should see about getting a door put on the entrance to those caves and keeping it locked. I am sure they are dangerous, and have told the doctor so many times."

"Aye, I'll speak to him about it," said MacGregor. I suspected he would not.

"Now," said Mrs McAllister to me, "I am come to luncheon. You cannot present yourself in the dining room in that state, so you had better go and change."

I resisted the temptation to say, "Yes, miss," as if she were one of my teachers. She seemed to assume that she was responsible for my behaviour in the absence of my mother. I wondered what sort of life her own daughter had led before her marriage. "Very well," I said, coolly enough to indicate my resentment but politely enough not to offend her. "May I ask, what time is luncheon?"

"We gather in the Great Hall at one o'clock."

MacGregor had disappeared around the corner of the house and Mrs McAllister fell into step with me as we approached the front door. "Doctor Hamish always comes in to luncheon if he has not been called away elsewhere, and I have a standing invitation," she added.

I digested this news. "So you do not live here at the castle?"

"I live at the Lodge," she informed me stiffly. The plumage on her hat caught the breeze as she nodded in the direction of the driveway that led down the hill. "Down there, beside the main gate. I attribute my good health to the walk between my wee house and the castle, which I take almost daily. Even in winter."

As we walked, she explained further. "My late husband was the vicar of St Matthew's in Stirling. After he died, when the new vicar needed the vicarage, Anne and I moved to a cottage in Drumwithie, because I had spent holidays in this part of Scotland as a girl, and was fond of it. When Anne and Hamish married, Hamish kindly invited me to moved into the Lodge."

We had reached the vestibule. With a nod to me, Mrs McAllister entered the Great Hall, and I set off up the stone stairs. I had no wish to meet anyone on the way to the tower room, so I hurried all the way there, taking the curving stairs two at a time and arriving at the top breathless. When I opened the door to my bedroom I almost cried out with shock. Jamie was sprawled on my bed, smoking.

An avalanche of indignation tore over me. "What are you doing here?" I demanded. "How can you show your face after what you did to me? Get off my bed and out of my sight!"

He did not move. On his face was an expression between bewilderment and contrition, as hungry for forgiveness as a child.

"Did you hear me?" Furious, I took hold of his ankle and tried to pull him off the bed. But he clamped his cigarette between his lips and clung to the bedstead with both hands.

"Look at me!" I persisted. "My dress is ruined, my boots are filthy and I was scared almost to death down there!" I let go of his ankle; it was fruitless to think I could manhandle him. I felt defeated. "Why did you leave me alone? And why did you smash the lantern? I couldn't find my way out of the caves – you *knew* I couldn't – so I ended up having to climb the ladder in that dirty, disgusting well! Do you wonder I am angry with you?"

His eyes glinted. There might have been tears in them or it might have been the reflection of the midday light from the tower windows. He took the cigarette out of his mouth. "I was cruel, wasn't I?"

"Yes, you were." I sat down on the dressing-stool and regarded him, my indignation evaporating. I felt relieved that he understood how much he had frightened me, and I also felt compassion, which was more difficult to explain. Surely *he* should be feeling compassion for *me*?

"I am very sorry, Cat," he said. "I do things like that sometimes. I am ..." – he sought a suitable word – "impulsive. My grandmother says my mother was the same at my age."

"I see." There was no time to ask him to explain further. I had to change my clothes and our elders awaited us downstairs. "Let us speak of it later. I have already encountered MacGregor, and Mrs McAllister, who scolded me for my appearance."

He still did not move. He lay there, the fingers of his left hand still curled around the bars of the bedstead, his hair as unruly as ever, his eyes fixed upon my face. "Do you forgive me?"

I tried to disguise my mixed feelings by shaking my head and sighing, in imitation of those very schoolteachers I despised. "We will speak of it later," I repeated.

He let go of the bedstead and sat up. Half-obscured by strands of golden hair, his eyes were wide. "I labour under an intolerable weight, knowing that a lifetime of unhappiness awaits me. If I do not do as my father wishes, I will lose Drumwithie. Can you wonder I am ill-tempered?"

I was surprised. "Surely your father has not threatened you with disinheritance?"

"Not directly," he admitted. "But he says he will not allow a man with no profession – *no profession*, Cat! – to live in idleness – *idleness! He has never tried to write a poem!* – in a place the family has maintained for generations. He is fond of asking me if I think Drumwithie pays for itself. He is so *intolerant*."

I was unmoved. "His intolerance, as you call it, does not explain why you behaved so badly today."

He laughed, blowing out a great cloud of cigarette smoke. "I was incensed by your insistence we leave the caves, when I did not want to," he said good-naturedly, waving at the smoke. "I believe it is called being spoilt."

This, at least, was honest. "So you consider yourself spoilt, then?"

"I consider myself spoilt beyond repair."

Being spoilt was one of the detestable shortcomings on my mother's long, and rather inconsistent, list. "You spoil that child, David!" she would cry if my father let me ride on his shoulders, or gave me a chocolate. But I was not spoilt; my lack of brothers and sisters never resulted in either of my parents over-indulging me. How different it had been for Jamie, though. Growing up in a castle, never going to school, petted by women, and all the time knowing he was heir to one of the most beautiful estates in Scotland.

"Your father treats you very sensibly," I said. "If you are spoilt, others are to blame."

He smoked in silence for a little while. I could see in the

expression of his eyes that scenes from the past were revisiting him. I said nothing and waited.

"I loved her to distraction. Mother, I mean. I still do. She was very beautiful. Here." He thrust his hand into his pocket and withdrew a small leather wallet, which he tossed onto the bed within my reach. "I have a photograph. It was taken before her illness became what it is today. She did not like the library or the Great Hall. This photograph was taken in the small drawing room, where she preferred to sit. Have you seen the portrait of her in there? My father commissioned it when they were first married."

I opened the wallet. The photograph showed a woman, past girlhood but not yet middle-aged, posed at the window of a room I had not yet seen. The dark foliage of a vase of peonies beside her contrasted with her white gown – an evening gown, the bodice and sleeves trimmed with lace, the skirt elaborately draped. Her dark hair was arranged in the style made popular by the late king's wife, Queen Alexandra, swept up at the back into an ornament and a "front" of curls above her brow. It was old-fashioned now, but it did not detract from the striking exquisiteness of her face. Light-eyed, with shapely brows and fine cheekbones, she gazed at the camera with the smallest of smiles on her lips. There was something of Mrs McAllister in the shape of her chin, but she had none of her mother's aloofness. She looked amiable, ready for conversation and hungry for friendship. The picture I had conjured of a tortured Ophelia could not have been more inaccurate.

I gazed at the photograph for a long time. Jamie had finished his cigarette and stubbed it out, and still I was looking at his mother. "She is certainly a beauty," I said at last. "And quite unlike how I imagined her. She is not like *my* mother at all, who is sort of pink and white, like a doll. Your mother is not doll-like at all. She is elegant and very lovely."

I stopped, aware that I had "rattled on" – another listed misdemeanour. "Forgive me," I said, looking up from the picture. "I was entranced."

"So was I, and remain so," he said. His tone was level, without emotion. "But the woman in this photograph has gone. She would not entrance anyone she met for the first time now." He looked at me sorrowfully. "You will not meet her, though. My father and grandmother sometimes visit her, but I have not been for a long time. I cannot bear the place she is in." His voice took on a plaintive tone. "And I am not convinced... I think visits do more harm than good. It is another thing Father and I argue about."

I handed him the wallet. As he put it in his pocket, his gaze dropped. "She will never come back," he whispered.

I did not do him the disservice of plying him with platitudes. Anne Buchanan was evidently seriously disturbed in her mind, and was in the best place, distressing though Jamie found it. "Now," I told him gently, "you must go, and I must change before I can face your father."

He stood up and crossed the room so quickly I hardly saw him move. "Will you allow me to watch with you tonight?"

he asked from the door. "In case the ghost returns? I have thought of nothing else since you told me."

I considered. "Do you do not think your presence may discourage it?"

"Let me watch anyway!" he implored. "I am too curious to stay away!"

I wondered whether allowing an evening visit by a young man to my private room was not a breach of propriety. I was sure it was, in fact. But Jamie's father and grandmother did not need to know about it, and I could not refuse – I was far too curious myself. "Very well, we will watch together tonight. Come at nine o'clock," I said, and closed the door after him.

The slime-covered walls of the well had streaked the bodice of my grey dress. I took it off and examined the stains, hoping Bridie was a skilled washerwoman. When I had put on another dress and washed my face, there still remained five minutes before I had to present myself downstairs. I sat down at the open window before the view I had already appropriated as mine. This morning, when I had first opened the curtains, a mist had obscured the glen and the distant mountains had been garlanded by clouds. But the breezy sunshine had dispelled the haze and the scene below me spread in colours brighter than any painter's brush could capture.

Tourists on their return home often described views they had seen as breathtakingly beautiful. My view truly was. I simply could not breathe normally as I looked at it. The glittering greens and greys, the bright shoots on the trees where birds sang all day long, the purple chasm of the glen below, the shadow of the castle itself – these sights brought my heart into my throat. Their beauty made me think of Jamie's poor mother, who could no longer live in the place which commanded such a view, though it was her home.

The clock struck the hour. They would be waiting. Reluctantly I left the room. When I reached the Great Hall, I put my ear to the door. The murmur of voices told me everyone else was present and I would have to make an entrance. "Imagine you are the Princess of Belgravia," Mother would tell me when I was younger, "who *expects* everyone to look at her. So, when everyone *does* look at you, you will not be surprised. And always pinch your cheeks before you turn the handle."

It was not until much later that I discovered the Princess of Belgravia was not a real person, but I invoked her memory now. I coughed by way of warning and opened the door.

"Ah, Catriona!" Doctor Hamish stood when I entered. "I hear you and Jamie have been exploring our caves! They are very fine, do you not agree?"

Jamie and his grandmother occupied the two fireside chairs, so I perched on the edge of a straight-backed chair. "Yes, indeed," I concurred. "Very fine."

"And very dark and very wet, and Jamie left you alone there, the scoundrel," said Jamie, who had an open book on his lap and did not look up. "But I have made it clear, Father, that I had an emergency – I will not offend Grandmother's sensibilities by detailing of what sort – and had to leave Cat. When I went back, she had found her own way out."

This was of course a lie, but I guiltily admired the ease with which Jamie told it. He had neither had an "emergency" nor returned to look for me. We both knew, however, that I would not contradict him.

"Jamie," said the doctor with a pained expression, "you must treat Catriona in a gentlemanly fashion. She is not a plaything provided for your entertainment."

Jamie's head did not move, but his downcast gaze slid sideways towards me. "No, she is the Cait Sìth, come to cast her spell on us."

Mrs McAllister's head came up. "Jamie!" She turned to me. "What has my grandson been telling you?"

"Oh … I asked him why he called me a cat, apart from my name being Catriona, that is, and he told me about the Cait Sìth." I glanced at Jamie. "He says I look like a cat and I have been sent from the supernatural world."

She stared at me blankly.

"He has romantic notions, I think," I added.

"I wonder if 'romantic' is the correct word for his notions!" snorted Doctor Hamish.

"The Cait Sìth is not a *notion*, romantic or otherwise," declared Mrs McAllister. "Catriona, I must make you familiar with other tales from Scottish folklore. You will not describe them as romantic, I assure you!"

There was a silence. Doctor Hamish took out his fob watch. "Where is Bridie? I have the devil of a hunger on me!"

"Luncheon will be ten minutes or more yet, Hamish," said Mrs McAllister. She turned again to me. For the first time since I had met her, there was a smile upon her lips. "Perhaps you would like to hear more about these tales? Though English people, having a folk culture considerably less rich than ours, usually dismiss Celtic beliefs as nonsense."

Ignoring this barb and hoping to please her, I nodded. "Yes, of course. I am sure they are fascinating."

"Then I will tell you of a legend as old as time itself. The deepest rooted and most persistent of all Scottish folklore. The story of the faerie child." She took off her spectacles and sat back in her chair, her expression softer than I had yet seen it. "It is believed," she began, "that some children, often oddly behaved ones, sickly ones, and so on, are not human at all, but faerie children, changelings, left by the faerie folk in exchange for the human child. In a household where a changeling has been left, a payment must be made by the fairies to the devil every seven years."

"What sort of payment?" I asked.

"It usually takes the form of a death or tragic occurrence in the human world," replied Mrs McAllister. "This sort of belief is present in folklore all over the world, as people seek a way to explain unhappy events. In Scotland it is known as the *teind*, Gaelic for "tithe", meaning a tenth part."

"I understand," I said. "About tithes, I mean." I had grown up in an agricultural area of midland England, surrounded by tenant farmers who followed the ancient practice of paying a tenth part of their profits to the parish. "And do people still believe this legend today?"

"Aye," nodded Mrs McAllister. "You will still see precautions taken against the stealing of a child, especially in the Highlands. Folk will leave scissors open where the child sleeps, or put a coat upside down over the cradle, particularly if the child is fair."

She paused and a silence fell. Jamie was deep in a book of poems and his father had the financial pages of *The Times* open; I was reluctant to break the spell Mrs McAllister's words had cast upon me. But although I half knew the answer, I asked, "Is a fair-haired child more likely to be taken, then?"

"Oh, yes! It is well known that the faeries are attracted by beautiful infants with blond hair."

She nodded towards her grandson. "Thank goodness, they have left ours alone, though Jamie's hair was pure white when he was a wee one!"

Doctor Hamish made a sound like "Hrmph!" He threw open the door and marched towards the dining room. "Bridie!" he called. "I can wait no longer! Bring me my luncheon!"

Mrs McAllister and I followed, and Jamie brought up the rear of our little procession. I was sure he was looking at the nape of my neck, where I had placed a tortoiseshell comb when I had piled up my hair. Self-conscious, I did what the Princess of Belgravia would have done. I walked serenely, trying not to think about who might be scrutinizing me, and attending to Mrs McAllister's small talk as if it were the most important thing in the world.

That evening I wrote to my mother. I asked her to send winter underwear and a woollen shawl. I had to reload my pen nib several times, as the ink kept drying while I tried to think of suitable words to describe Jamie. In the end I told her that he was striking-looking, intelligent and mercurial. I did not tell her, however, that he and his father were at loggerheads. I told her that Mrs McAllister was an enthusiastic regulator of my behaviour, but not that I resented this. I was perfectly truthful about the hospitality of Doctor Hamish and gave her brief descriptions of Bridie and MacGregor. I told her about my room in the tower, my glorious view and Anne's Garden, but not about the caves or what had happened there. And I certainly did not mention the other-worldly screams and the girl in the ragged dress. When I could think of no more to write, I went downstairs and left the envelope on the table by the front door, where the doctor had told me to leave letters for MacGregor to post.

Dusk – the gloaming, as they call it in Scotland – was falling on Drumwithie. Clouds had gathered in the late afternoon and spots of rain had fallen on my window as I dressed for dinner. I had put on my only evening dress, of brown silk. It had a square neck, a straighter skirt than I wore in the daytime and a crêpe-de-Chine waistband that required stiffening with uncomfortable canvas stays. I had even made an attempt to curl my hair. But when I reached the dining room I realized I should not have bothered. Bridie had served the doctor, Jamie and me with cold venison sandwiches, pickled beetroot and a dish of lettuce and tomatoes. A bowl of fruit, from which both men helped themselves to apples and oranges, was the only dessert. Luncheon, evidently, was the main meal in this house. It was a long time since this traditional pattern of meals had been current at Chester House; we always ate sparingly at luncheon and "dressed" in the evening.

I was embarrassed, but not surprised. Doctor Hamish had had the tact not to mention my appearance and Jamie had produced a sound like "Hrrzzah!", which could have meant anything, but I admonished myself for not predicting what Mrs McAllister's regular presence at luncheon signified. The doctor, whose profession required early starts, late returns on horseback, and an active day's work in between, needed a good meal at midday. Anticipating another meal in the evening, at luncheon I had not eaten as much as I wanted of the excellent leek soup and chicken pie. Tomorrow, I would know better.

All this went through my mind as I returned to the tower room. My writing things lay scattered on the table; I tidied them away. The blouse I had taken off, but would wear again tomorrow, hung on the outside of the wardrobe; I put it inside. My boots, which I had forgotten to take to the boot room, were in two different parts of the room; I set them together by the hearth. I poked the fire. I went to draw the curtains, but when I saw the magnificent colours of the sky, I left them open. Then I turned up the lamp and set it in the middle of the table.

There was nothing left to do, so I sat down nervously in the armchair by the fire. I wished Jamie would come soon – it was five to nine, earlier than I had seen the vision last night, but darkness was falling quickly. I could see a clear reflection of the pool of lamplight in the window. I stared at it, my ears straining to hear either a woman's voice or a knock at my door.

I heard neither. But I did hear something else. At first I was unsure what the soft whooshing could be. I sat forward, listening, growing more fearful as the sound gathered momentum. It came to me suddenly that it must be the whipping of a wind, the sort of deep-winter wind that sweeps the landscape at the beginning of a storm. But the curtains hung perfectly still at the open window. The wind was something unreal.

Then came another sound, layered within the storm. A sound as familiar to a girl from farming country as the wind-wail. It was the raucous, unearthly cackle of a pack of crows. I could hear the birds as plainly as if they were under my open window. Rising cautiously, I put my head out, expecting an increase in the birds' sounds, to find them sitting on a nearby tree. But no trees grew near the tower.

Fear overcame me. Almost ready to faint, I collapsed again on the armchair and covered my face with my hands. "Stop!" I shouted, as loudly as I could. "Please, please, stop!" I had no regard for anyone who might hear me or what conclusion they might draw. My only thought was to obliterate the noise by making a louder noise myself. "Leave me alone!" I pleaded. "I beg you, leave me be!"

My ears were assailed for a few more moments. Then, suddenly, silence fell. I peeked between my fingers. I stood and turned full circle, alert for any noise or movement , but there was none. The room was empty. The circle of lamplight on the table, the boots by the fire, all was recognizable as ordinary, comforting real life. Yet I knew I had not been deceived, even though darkness and apprehension could play tricks on the nerves, and I *had* been nervous, up here in this oddly fashioned room, waiting for Jamie's knock.

"Jamie!" I opened the door wide, and called down the passage. There was no reply. I ran to the top of the stairs and leaned over the banister. "Jamie! Jamie, are you there?"

I heard his footsteps on the landing and his yellow head appeared at the bottom of the spiral staircase, his face turned upwards in alarm. "What is it? What has happened? Are you all right?"

"Will you come up? There is something up here! Well, it has gone now, but I definitely heard something!"

While I was babbling he was bounding up the stairs. "The vision, you mean? Did you see the vision? Damn! I've missed it!"

He was babbling as much as I was. "Jamie, I did not see the vision," I told him as we entered the tower room. "I heard the sound of a high wind, and then … it was so loud, it seems scarcely possible, but there was the noise of crows."

He was so surprised, he had to steady himself by gripping the back of a chair. *"What?"*

"Crows. I know what they sound like because—"

"Cat, do you know what you are saying?" He looked at me with a mixture of fear, wonder and triumph. "A gathering of crows is a sign of death!"

I stared at him and he stared back at me, his eyes alight. "Do you not think I am right to be concerned?"

"I do not know what to think." I tried to compose myself. "It is too strange to understand. Before I entered this room last night I would have dismissed stories of the faerie folk and the Cait Sìth as nonsense. But you are convinced that these weird noises and this phantom girl have been conjured by my presence. That is such a frightening thought! Do you think they mean to hurt me?"

Jamie sat down in the armchair. Careless of my best dress, I knelt on the hearthrug at his feet. Outside the still-open curtains, night had descended on the glen. I could hear the cooing of a wood pigeon, far away in some lofty tree. The world was silent, ready for sleep. But the world reflected in the window was not. The firelight cast weird shapes on the walls; the air felt smoky and close; my heart beat unsteadily in my breast.

"No, I do not," said Jamie, looking into the fire. "I think they have come to you for help."

"But what can I do?" I was bewildered. "If the girl is dead, what can anybody do?"

"We must wait and see. She will come again, but not when I am here." He looked at me with his glittering look. "The crows must have been sent to warn me off. I think only *you* must watch, Cat. Every night, alone."

1896

Fourteen years previously

*B*eyond the castle windows, spring was taking hold of Drumwithie. It was the first week of April. The air was mild and sweetened by a soft breeze bearing the scent of flowers. Last year at this time she had walked in the grounds while the boy ran about, coming to her with treasures – a pine cone, a raven's feather, a smooth pebble. She and her husband had made an excursion to Ben Nevis, the highest mountain in Scotland. But this year she could only imagine the breeze, and the boy's delighted cries, and the scent of the flowers. She was too ill to go out.

She lay on the sofa in her favourite room, the small drawing room that led off the Great Hall. It had smaller windows than the library, where her husband liked to sit, but she preferred the view. It was Saturday and the boy was free from lessons, but she did not know where he was; he had not visited her this morning. His father had probably taken him to Drumwithie, where everyone knew him. According to her husband, the stonemason's wife had whispered a warning on her recent visit to the surgery. "Ye'll have to watch that boy, Doctor. He has the look of the faeries on him."

Educated people had no time for such village superstition, of course. But the thought of the woman's words troubled her. A golden-haired, green-eyed child. Sometimes, when the light caught the boy's eyes in a certain way, they had the cast of other-worldliness on them. But a moment later, he would be her affectionate, seven-year-old darling again and she would shake such nonsense from her mind.

She glanced at the fire in the grate. It was no longer roaring as it had been when Bridie had lit it this morning, but it still glowed red. A wild thought came to her: could memories be burned? What would she have to burn, to free herself? With trembling fingers she tore a scrap of lace from the trimming of her sleeve – it came away easily; she had been meaning to ask Bridie to oversew the fraying seam – and tossed it onto the coals, where it immediately flared. Its ashes were an obliteration. If she burned not only the lace from her sleeve, but the sleeve itself, the house gown, everything in this room … would the memories they contained be obliterated too? Or would the whole exercise be futile? This poison was in her head, borne silently for so long, and would only be destroyed if she were to destroy herself.

Her eyes travelled to the portrait above the mantelpiece. A picture of her, yet not of her. Of a young woman who had married Hamish Buchanan and come to Drumwithie full of hope. Her mother had considered the match a triumph. What did she herself consider it? A prison sentence of the worst kind, when the prisoner does not know how many years she has left to serve?

I KNOW
WHO I LOVE

Between nine and ten o'clock the next night, I made sure I was alone in the tower room. I watched and listened until the fire had died and the window showed nothing but blackness. But no voice came and no ghostly figure appeared. The same happened the next night and the one after that. When I had been at the castle a week, I gave up expecting any more visitations.

"I must have been mistaken," I told Jamie. "I feel very foolish."

He was scornful. "How could you be mistaken? You heard it and you saw it."

"It might have been a trick."

His scorn increased. "A *trick*? Who would play such a trick? And how could they do it? Be reasonable, Cat."

"I *am* being reasonable." His condescension was making me feel worse. I was irritable enough to swipe at an unsuspecting branch of broom, scattering its yellow flowers. I had found Jamie in the garden. Not Anne's Garden, but further from the house, in the untamed tangle MacGregor professed to be "trimming" whenever I saw him there, but which never showed any sign of improvement. Broom, heather and gorse encroached freely on it from the hillside, and the only discernible path was becoming more overgrown as the hours of daylight increased.

"It is not reasonable to change your mind so completely in the course of a week," insisted Jamie. He grinned suddenly. "Anyone would think you were a *girl*."

"You are so funny, you should go on the stage." I sounded moody. I *felt* moody. I had been unsettled for days, anxious in case I saw the bedraggled girl again, more anxious because I did not.

"Cat…" Jamie stopped, but he was behind me and I walked on, oblivious. "*Cat!* Listen to me!"

I turned. For a moment I thought something had happened to my eyesight, making the landscape shimmer like an image in a dream. But what I saw was real. Jamie, who was clad in his usual ensemble of unconnected garments, stood in the knee-high undergrowth, a switch of gorse in his hand. He looked like a reaper in a cornfield. It was the late afternoon of a cloudless day and the sun had almost disappeared around the corner of the house. Jamie was standing where the shadow bisected the garden, half in and half out of the sun. Its rays landed a glancing blow on his hair, burnishing it to an even brighter gold. And behind him, rising perpendicular to the rock, taller from this angle than any other, loomed the ruined castle. So many colours played on its walls that I thought of Lord Tennyson's famous lines, "The splendour falls on castle walls", and rejoiced that I was alive to see what was spread before me. A beautiful place, a beautiful sky. And, I realized, a beautiful young man.

"I am sorry," he said. He was standing with his back to the light and I could not see his expression, but his tone was contrite. "I was facetious. But, please, do not doubt yourself. The spirit will walk again, when it chooses."

"Supposing it does not, in the whole time I am here?"

"It *will*."

"How do you know that?"

"I just do." He began to walk towards me, and as he came into the shade I saw the earnestness in his face. "Believe me, it will."

"Because I am the Cait Sìth? Because of the gift you say I have?"

He had reached me. He stood close enough for me to smell the perspiration in his shirt and the smoke in his hair. It was not a combination I cared for and I stepped back. But he stepped closer again. "Do not dismiss it," he told me firmly. "We are mortal. Our time in the earthly world is short. But our spirits go on for ever – it is not only the Christian religion that teaches this – and some do not rest until they find peace. This is a restless spirit that is speaking to you and you must not deny it its moment. Do you promise you will not give up?"

I nodded. I did not understand his conviction, but I could see I must honour it. "Of course. I will go on watching, every night."

"Very well." He looked at the ground, swishing the gorse switch. "I will trust you to do so. And *you* must trust that she will come back."

We began to walk back towards the house. I fell into step beside him, struggling with a purposeless sort of agitation. Apprehension about this "restless spirit", certainly, but more than apprehension. There was a tight feeling between my waist and my chest, as if a spring had been wound up and held firm, ready for the moment of release. But the moment did not come. All the way back through the wilderness, and then the neat part of the garden, over the bridge and round the corner to the boot room door, through the passageway to the Great Hall, the spring remained wound. Jamie strolled beside me carelessly. But I was more aware of his presence than I had ever been aware of anything. My senses had jumbled themselves up and settled again, as randomly as the pieces of coloured glass in a kaleidoscope. I could not tell which of them was responsible for my excited state, nor which aspect of Jamie had given rise to it.

Girls at school had described their crushes, usually on friends of their brothers or on Herr Steiger, our German tutor, who had the double distinction on the school staff of being male and under forty. They would say their corset would feel too tight when the object of desire came into view or even into mind, and their heart would beat fast, and they would feel cold, but perspire in an unladylike way. Blushing also loomed large.

No boy had ever inspired anything in me but mild friendship, usually short-lived. But something about Jamie had communicated itself to me in that moment when I had turned to him in the sunlight. I tried to breathe deeply, as my mother always told me to when I felt nervous, but found I could not fill my lungs. My heart had expanded so much it had crushed them.

Jamie seemed preoccupied and I was grateful for his silence. I was also thankful that there remained half an hour until suppertime. I would have time to calm myself before I sat down opposite him at the table.

In my room I washed hurriedly, and tied up my hair, then let it down again. The mirror did not show me the serenity I hoped for, but a solemn mouth and excited eyes. I tried smiling; it did not look sincere. I tried to tranquillize the expression of my eyes; it was impossible.

I changed my clothes. Not into my evening dress, which had hung abandoned in the cupboard since my second night at the castle, but into my dark skirt and favourite navy blue blouse. I liked the plain cotton the blouse was made of, the neat fit of the sleeves and the modest, pin-tucked front. The collar was not stiff, but surrounded my throat comfortably. It was plainer than anything my mother or her friends would wear, but I considered its lack of decoration elegant. I brushed my hair, loosely securing the front away from my brow with combs and leaving the sides free to swing over my cheeks. As I put the brush down I heard a woman's voice.

For a nerve-racking moment I thought it was my invisible visitor. But no. This woman was singing contentedly and the sound was coming in through the half-open window. Cautiously, I opened the window further and put my head out.

Bridie was in the kitchen yard below the tower. She was wearing a sacking apron, and beside her stood a bucket of soapy water. As she scrubbed the cobbles with a broom, she sang a simple song to a simple tune.

> *"I know where I'm going,*
> *And I know who's going with me.*
> *I know who I love,*
> *And the dear knows who I'll marry.*
> *Some say he's poor,*
> *But I say he's bonny,*
> *The fairest of them all,*
> *My handsome winsome Johnny."*

I gripped the window frame. *I know who I love.* The fairest of them all. Handsome, winsome.

If ever there was a word for Jamie's fear of future unhappiness, his disarming confession of an indulged life, his susceptibility to mysticism and his disordered, green–gold appearance, it was *winsome*.

"Feather beds are soft,
And painted rooms are bonny,
But I would leave them all
To go with my love Johnny."

I listened in wonder, feeling suspended between heaven and earth, between now and the future. Great happiness and great uncertainty flooded over me. Did I know where I was going?

As soon as I opened the dining-room door I could see that Jamie and his father were arguing.

"The medical profession is a calling, like the priesthood," Jamie was saying, his voice filled with frustration. "A calling which I do not possess. And furthermore, I have no wish to engage in a profession that is full of quacks!"

"Unfortunately," retorted the doctor impatiently, "sick people are desperate and often they can afford neither a qualified doctor's bills nor the education needed to know their condition is incurable!"

"So that is what you believe, is it? That Mother's condition is incurable? So why do you employ the quacks?"

Doctor Hamish flushed. "Jamie, that is unfair! You know perfectly well I was speaking generally!"

Jamie was hunched in his chair, his elbow on the table and his bony shoulders raised. I thought how like a petulant child he looked. "It is, though, is it not?" he said accusingly. "She will never get better. She will die in that horrible place."

I was waiting in the doorway, unwilling to interrupt. Doctor Hamish, whose good manners would not allow him to sit until I had arrived, gripped the back of the carver's chair, his face pinched. When he saw me, he attempted a smile. "Good evening, Catriona. We have Finnan Haddie this evening. Do you like smoked haddock?"

"I think so." I was not sure. At Chester House fish was usually served as an appetizer, in the form of small rolls of salmon or potted shrimps. "But I'm sure it will be very good."

The doctor sat down, shook out his napkin and took the lid off the serving dish in front of him. His anger was plain, but courtesy prevented him from admonishing his son outright in front of me. "Jamie," he said, ladling my portion onto a plate, "surely you understand how privileged you are?"

"Privileged!" Jamie pushed his hair back and frowned. "Father, I have done everything I can to please you, studying for those wretched examinations in subjects quite uninteresting to me, but I cannot – I *cannot* enter the Medical School next term. The idea simply repels me." He let go of his hair and looked at me earnestly through the forelock. "Cutting up corpses! Learning by rote the names of every particle of the human body, every revolting ailment! Can you imagine it, Cat!"

I could, and at the same time could not, imagine it. Doctor

Hamish was correct; Jamie was privileged. Before him lay a life that could not be more different from that of the heiress to Graham's Wholesome Foods. Watching his excited face, I silently repeated a catechism of his privileges. Male. Well educated. Heir to an extensive estate. Shortly to be on his way to the city, to go to university, to train as a doctor like his father, to be a doctor...

"Actually," I said calmly, "I am in agreement with your father." I accepted the plate the doctor handed me. Finnan Haddie was a milky-looking fish stew. It smelled strong. "It *is* a privilege, and a fascinating one, to study medicine."

Jamie was newly bathed and shaven, and dressed artistically in a loose tunic with a silk scarf at his neck. His eyes roamed over my face as he took his own plate. "You have not put up your hair," he said blankly.

I avoided his gaze, aware my cheeks had gone pink. "Do not change the subject. Studying is privilege enough, but surely university life brings other pleasures too. I know little about it, but I suspect you will make lifelong friends among the other young men, who will have much in common with you."

"And young women too!" The doctor spoke lightly, looking at me with amusement and a hint of pride. "Did you know that Edinburgh is one of the most enlightened universities in the world, Catriona? The number of female students in the Medical School grows every year."

I was too amazed to answer him. Who were these women

whose destiny led them to become doctors? How wondrous and thrilling to do such a thing! "Can women be doctors, then?" I asked at last. "Surely not! I mean, I have never heard of any."

"Their degrees are not at present recognized," he explained. "Though some of them do practise, privately, particularly in the field of women's health." He was looking at me intently and stabbed the air with his fork as he spoke. "But I am fully convinced that not only will women gain the vote they are at present agitating for, they eventually *will* be awarded recognized degrees and will enter the medical profession on an even footing with men. Indeed, it is my personal belief that they will make exceptionally fine doctors. Of course, the Prime Minister will pontificate and pompous fools will write to *The Times*, but progress will come without a doubt." He paused to take a mouthful. When he had swallowed it, he added, "It is clear to me that any right-thinking person understands that women's minds are the equal of men's and the only reason women do not fill the pages of history books is their lack of opportunity to do so."

I had never heard such words from a man. Incredulous, I turned to Jamie. "What do *you* think?"

He shrugged, intent on his fish. "What Father says is so obvious I do not consider it a worthy subject for reflection."

"So Jamie and I agree on something, you see!" observed Doctor Hamish. "The world has changed a great deal in this new century, Catriona, and it will change more. The belief is growing that the ambitions of intelligent young people of *both* sexes should be encouraged."

I thought about my grandmother, moving through the nineteenth century as serenely as Queen Victoria herself. I thought about my parents, who had been young when the Queen had died, and had lived these ten rather heady years of the new century under King Edward's indulgent rule. They had allowed me to attend school instead of having a governess. They had given me a bicycle, and a schoolfriend had taught me the new style of energetic dancing, which we had practised to the gramophone her brother had brought back from Cambridge. Gilchester was full of cricket-playing, wager-laying, pub-frequenting young men, who seemed bent on enjoying life to the full, with little consistent income and no apparent ambition. King Edward's son George was now on the throne, and *Times* columnists were already calling this the "New Georgian" age. What, I wondered, would the next few years bring for us New Georgians?

We continued to eat in silence. The haddock was more palatable than I had feared, but I ate slowly. Jamie put down his fork, picked up his wine glass, sat back and addressed me. "So, Cat, you consider me privileged. But what would you do if *you* were in my situation?"

I hesitated, wondering how to frame a reply that would not offend either of them.

"You have not made yourself clear, Jamie," said Doctor Hamish. He tore a piece of bread and dipped it into his sauce.

"Are you asking Catriona what she would do if she were a man of twenty-one who has earned a place to study medicine, or herself?"

I felt Jamie's eyes on my skin, my cotton blouse and my loosened hair. "Herself," he said.

"Then I could never be in your situation." I tried to keep my tone light, though a familiar resentment was rising. "I am a girl, so it did not occur to my father to provide me with the kind of education that leads to a university. I need not worry about what to do in order to support my dependants. I am a dependant myself."

"Why, you have made me wish I were a girl!" cried Jamie. "There would be no arguments with my father and no discussion about inheritance. I would be destined to marry a man who would keep me for the rest of my days." He smiled, delighted by a new thought. "And if I were to write poetry, everyone would admire me! 'How clever she is!' they would say. 'How accomplished! And we thought she could only do needlework and instruct the servants!'"

"Do not joke, Jamie," said Doctor Hamish. "Catriona is in earnest. Tell me, my dear, did you quarrel with your father about this?"

"No, never. I knew argument was futile. He used to say 'men organize the world and women do not need to know anything about it'."

"Then with the greatest respect to David's memory," said the doctor steadily, "he was quite wrong."

115

Speaking Father's words made them sound in my head. I longed beyond reason to be with him again. I placed my knife and fork together; I could not eat any more. "He was a man of his times, I think," I said, "whereas you are a man ahead of them. Perhaps if I were your daughter, I would be allowed to make my own way in the world and only marry if I really want to."

Aware that my face had turned very red, I shrank into my chair, drawing my skirt close and feeling foolish. "I'm sorry," I said, "now you know what a mean, dissatisfied little vixen I am."

Jamie's eyes travelled tolerantly over my face. His expression was not, to my relief, patronizing. But I waited apprehensively. He was like a firecracker; there was no telling in which direction he might bounce next. "Perhaps, then," he said gently, "you and I should change places. I will go and annoy your mother, and you can stay here and charm my father." He tilted his head towards the doctor. "How about it, Father? Would you not rather have an obedient daughter than a disobedient son?"

The doctor was about to speak, but his eyes drifted to the door, which was creaking ajar. "Ah!" he said, which he always did when servants appeared. "Coffee!"

Bridie entered, set the tray on the table, bobbed and left.

"Shall we take the coffee into the small drawing room?" suggested the doctor, pushing back his chair. "The sunset will be fine tonight. Jamie, carry the tray."

The west-facing drawing room contained Jamie's mother's image in two forms – the painting above the mantle and, in a silver frame on a table, a larger version of the photograph he carried in his wallet. There were several chairs and a low sofa, where I suspected she had often lain during her periods of illness. Walnut furniture and vases of fresh flowers made the room so attractive, it was obvious to my eyes why it was her favourite. If I were mistress of Drumwithie, it would be my favourite too.

When I had seated myself at one end of the sofa, Doctor Hamish offered the cigarette box to Jamie, who refused. The doctor took a cigarette himself and stood at the window, smoking absently and watching the pink- and yellow-streaked sky.

I looked at the coffee tray Jamie had left by the hearth. I had never tasted coffee. Here at the castle I had so far refused it after supper, and at home we always had tea or cocoa. "May I have some coffee tonight?" I asked the doctor. "I would like to try it, though Mother considers it bad for the digestion."

He laughed. "It may well be! But I will add plenty of cream and sugar."

"Thank you."

He prepared the coffee and handed it to me. I sipped. It was hot, sweet and delicious. "I like it!" I declared and they laughed.

"Splendid!" said Jamie, leaning forward to take his own coffee from the tray. "Coming to supper with your hair down, trying Finnan Haddie and drinking coffee! What new experience will be next, I wonder?"

The doctor said nothing. Jamie's eyes burned me; I lowered mine, not in modesty, but in mortification. He knew of my love. Of course he knew.

That night, the girl in the ragged silk dress revisited me.

I stayed up as late as I could, knowing I would not sleep easily. Jamie went into the library after supper, saying he wished to write. To be out of his company made me feel shamelessly disappointed. I sat with Doctor Hamish in the small drawing room for the rest of the evening, until he began to put lamps out and lock doors, and I had no choice but to bid him goodnight and come up to my room. I was not the smallest bit sleepy. Did drinking coffee stimulate the brain? I had a vague recollection that this was another of Mother's objections to it, a stimulated mind not being desirable in a manageable daughter.

Upstairs, I sat another hour in my favourite place by the window, breathing the pine-laden air. There were no clouds and the moonlight gave the landscape a two-dimensional aspect, with objects and their shadows picked out in shades of grey, like a photograph. An owl hooted and another responded from a different part of the wood. It was a comforting sound, reminding me that other creatures apart from myself were awake, yet an eerie one, an invisible lament from the darkness. I recalled my English mistress reading us something about "the witching hour" of night.

Remembering this fragment of poetry brought my thoughts to Jamie and the scene I had witnessed at the supper table. He and his father were both strong-willed; I could not predict which of them would win the struggle. Perhaps neither. I hoped Doctor Hamish might allow Jamie to go to the University as planned, but study something other than medicine, and follow a different profession, more conducive to his interest in poetry. But it was not my quarrel. I could not take sides or make suggestions. All I hoped for was that they would both, in the end, be content.

Midnight struck. I closed the window against the chill air, changed into my nightdress, turned out the lamp and got into bed. I lay there for what seemed like a long time, watching the fire die. And then, with no warning and no sound, the darkness of the room seemed to fold in upon itself, like curtains in the theatre drawing back to reveal a lighted stage. She was there: my visitor with the tumbling hair and the dirty pink frock.

I did not mean to move, but my body stiffened involuntarily. Jamie was correct; I had the power to draw her, and when she wished to, she appeared. Trying not to make a sound, I watched her walk from the end of my bed to the window, where she sat down in the chair I had vacated. When she turned from the window and her eyes sought mine, as they had done before, I was convinced that she grieved for a loss. All ghosts grieve for their own death. And they return because something, some uncompleted quest, is drawing them back. But this girl's countenance showed suffering more than death itself.

She looked away again, towards the window. The moonlight shone, but she was insubstantial and cast no shadow. I gazed and gazed, terrified yet thrilled, wondering if she had appeared because she had something to say, something to plead for, or confess, or rid herself of. Something had brought her to my presence and no one else's. When her dark eyes looked at me, they told me, "I know you and you know me."

I did feel as if I knew her. We had things in common. She was near my age and her features were similar to those of mine that had made Jamie liken me to a cat. Dark, with a pale face and almond-shaped eyes. Just as he had said, it seemed she had languished somewhere for a long time, frozen in the moment of her death, until I had entered the tower room. Longing to be free, she sought my help.

She stood and leaned towards the windowpane. Her movements were graceful, like those of any slender girl, yet they were at the same time spectral, inhuman. I could feel myself shaking as I went on staring. She placed her palms against the glass and her forehead between them. Then she backed away and pointed to a place higher up the window. I followed her finger to the centre pane. What could she mean, pointing there? I could not ask her, but I hoped her expression might give me a clue. When I looked back at her, she was no longer there.

I threw back the bedclothes, scrambled out of bed and ran to the window. I was not tall enough to see out of the centre pane directly, and neither had the ghostly girl been. I dragged a chair under the window and stood on it, looking eagerly through the middle pane, my hands cupping my face. Disappointment stabbed me. There was nothing there.

I continued to look, straining for the sight of anything – a shrieking woman, crows, the girl herself – but the tower room window was very high, higher than the trees. As my eyes grew used to the darkness, I became more and more convinced that darkness was all there was. I stood there, indecisive. Then it came to me what I must do. I got down, flung my house robe over my nightdress and tied the sash with trembling fingers. Impropriety or no impropriety, I would go to Jamie's room.

The winding stairs creaked as I crept down them. I had never noticed it in the daytime. No matter where on each tread I stepped, it creaked. I hoped that by this time everyone in the house would be too deeply asleep to hear. I sped along the lower landing to the door at the end, which I knew led to Jamie's private sitting room. I had been in it once, to borrow a book.

It was small, with a casement window looking onto the courtyard at the rear of the castle, and the same high ceiling as the first-floor landing that led to it. The door was arched like all the castle doors, with an iron ring for a handle, which operated an old-fashioned latch of the kind seen on outdoor gates. In the daytime, the room was warmed by a good fire and cosy in a masculine way, with a patterned rug, untidy piles of books and a sofa with a blanket thrown over it, perhaps to hide its shabbiness. At night, it was a shadowy obstacle course.

I had never been in Jamie's bedroom, of course, and had been shocked when he had turned up in mine, even in the middle of the day. But here I was, making my way towards his door in the middle of the night. And undressed. What would Mother have said?

My shin struck something that turned out to be a footstool, and I cried out. There would be a bruise there tomorrow. I stood with my hand over my mouth and my eyes watering, waiting for the pain to lessen. And that was how Jamie found me when he opened the bedroom door.

"Cat!" His wary expression turned into surprise. "What on earth are you doing?"

I felt my way to the sofa and sat down, rubbing my shin. "She came again!"

We were both hissing in exaggerated whispers, though Doctor Hamish slept three thick-walled rooms away, and Bridie above the kitchen yard. Jamie fetched a dressing-gown from his bedroom and came back with it loose around his shoulders. As he moved closer I could make out that he looked tousled, and was blinking in sleepy astonishment. "Good God, what did you do?"

"Nothing. I was in bed and suddenly she was there."

122

"Are you sure you saw her?" He took a box of matches off the mantelpiece, lit the lamp and turned the flame low. The room was still shadowed, but now the gloom had a yellowish tinge. I saw that Jamie's dressing-gown had peacocks in full plumage embroidered on it.

"Of course I'm sure. But there is more, Jamie. Listen."

"I am listening." He threw the spent match into the grate and sat down on the arm of the sofa, his face looking thin and hollow in the lamplight.

"She gazed at me, with such … I don't know, longing, pleading," I told him. "She went to the window and laid her forehead against it, and then came away again and pointed at the middle pane. You know there are nine panes in that window? It was the middle one in the middle row. What do you think she meant by doing that?"

I knew I was gabbling, but I could not stop, and continued before he had a chance to speak. "She wants our help. Or, at least, my help. I could see it in her eyes. Oh, Jamie, I was so frightened!"

He put his hand on my arm. "Tell me again about the window."

"She pointed at the middle pane, then she disappeared. I went and looked, but there was nothing there."

"Perhaps if we look in daylight, we will see what she wants us to see."

"But the room is so high!" I could not help sounding impatient. "Outside the window there is only the sky!"

Through the thin material of my robe, I could feel his fingers encircling my arm. He did not seem inclined to remove his hand. In fact, he took hold of my other arm with his other hand, slid off the arm onto the seat of the sofa and pulled me towards him. I held my breath. "Cat, do you not see?" He was no longer whispering, though his voice was low. "That window overlooks the glen, where there is nothing but trees. So it must be something to do with a *tree*."

His eyes gleamed softly in the half-light. I had never been so close to a boy before. I tried to answer him, but could not find my breath. He moved even closer and gazed into my face with such tenderness, my heart leapt. My body seemed to melt under his touch. All my senses were heightened, all my sensations exaggerated, as if every nerve had been laid bare. Without questioning anything, I laid my head in the place between his chin and his shoulder, which fitted it exactly. His arms closed around my waist and we sat there in an impromptu, but not an awkward, embrace.

He squeezed me so tightly, I could feel the muscles in his arms and his ribs against mine. His chin rested on my forehead and he breathed quickly into my hair. "Cat," he said softly, "do you ... do you like me?"

I could not speak; my breath would not come. He moved closer, so that our foreheads were almost touching. "I mean, really like me?"

My heart was so full I said nothing for a moment. His presence overwhelmed me; I was as helpless as a doll. But I no longer felt his breath. He was holding it, waiting anxiously for my reassurance.

"Jamie…" I turned my face up to meet his gaze. "I do not know the words to tell you what I feel. But I know that my feelings are real."

He bent his head and kissed me swiftly, then pulled away and held me at arm's length. His face was alight with joy. "You are a beautiful and extraordinary person, my darling Cat," he said. "And if you would only give me the word, I will be your slave for ever."

Wild and whirling words! And typical of Jamie, of course – melodramatic and poetic. "You would make a sorry sort of slave," I said. "I would rather you cared for me as an equal, as I care for you."

"You care for me!" he echoed joyously. "I will care for you always!"

The lamp had almost run out of oil. Jamie's shaggy hair was an irregular shape against the moonlight from the window and I could no longer distinguish his features. I clung to him and he to me, and we kissed again, with more purpose. His lips felt warm and surprisingly soft. Drowning, submerged by this unexpected plunge into love, I kissed him and allowed myself to be kissed, over and over again.

Then, suddenly, I felt self-conscious. I was in his room, I was not wearing my corset or underclothes, and everyone else was asleep. Reluctantly, I began to disentangled myself. "Jamie, I should go."

His hands still held both mine. "I will not be able to go to sleep, after this."

"Neither will I." I stood up and pulled my robe close. "But you must agree, I have to go."

He opened the door. "Tomorrow, we will find what the ghost was pointing at," he whispered.

"I hope so."

We parted slowly, hands touching until the very last. "Goodnight," he said, kissing me once more.

My blood was still moving round my veins absurdly quickly. When I had turned the sitting room's iron latch silently behind me, I hurried up the spiral staircase, in the irrational hope that speed would lessen its creaking. It did not. My room seemed cold, and I huddled beneath the bed-clothes in my dressing-gown. When warmth did not come, I realized I was not cold at all, but shivering with excitement and intoxicated with love.

THE TREE

T he events of the night flooded back as soon as I awoke. Still heavy-headed from the short sleep I had eventually had, I rose and went to the window. It was another bright May morning. The air was clear, the dew was still on the grass and the landscape sparkled with the bright greens and yellows that only early summer can bring. I glanced at the clock; a quarter past seven. Everything was perfectly still. No branch trembled on the trees below my tower, and beyond, farther across the glen and into the purple of the mountains' shadow, the world lay expectantly, poised for the new day under the wide, unclouded sky.

Had it really happened? Had the ghostly visitor pointed out the middle pane? Had I rushed downstairs in my night-dress? Had Jamie and I embraced in his untidy sitting room, kissing? I hugged the thought to my heart, astonished.

There was a knock on my door. Thinking it must be Jamie, I rushed to open it. But Bridie stood there, as she did every morning at this time, bringing my hot water and ready to lay and light the fire. I backed towards the bed, found my robe and dragged it on. "Good morning, Bridie."

"Good day to ye, miss," she said in her modest way. She set down the ewer and knelt in front of the grate. I opened the wardrobe. "This is in need of a good brushing," I said, holding up my dark skirt and inspecting the hem. "Would you be so good as to—"

"To be sure, miss!" She was on her feet and taking the skirt from my hands. "Will there be anything else I may do for ye?"

I had never had a personal maid, but I had watched Susan wait upon my mother. "No, not now, thank you." There were other fires to light and breakfasts to get. "But before supper tonight, if you have time, will you come up and help me do my hair? I can never get it right, and I wish to look as nice as possible at table and for the evening afterwards."

Her brown eyes brightened and softened at the same instant. "Aye, miss, I'll do that gladly! And if ye have a blouse or a nightie to mend, or shoes to polish, give them to me and I'll see to them!"

"Thank you, Bridie." I took out my striped cotton dress and closed the wardrobe. "Now, you had better get on."

I washed and dressed as quickly as I could, while Bridie swept the already-spotless grate and set a match to the kindling she had laid. She had only just left and I was still fastening my belt, when Jamie knocked. Without waiting for an invitation, he came in, crossed the room and gave me an affectionate kiss on the cheek, as if I were a wife and he a husband arriving home from the office.

"This is what parents do!" I exclaimed.

"*My* parents don't." He went to the window overlooking the glen. "The middle pane?"

I nodded. "You will have to stand on the chair."

He climbed up, studied the view for a moment, then made room beside him on the chair and beckoned to me. "Tell me what you see."

I scrambled onto the chair. Jamie put his arm around my waist and held me tightly. "Can't have you falling off," he said solemnly. I was possessed of a desire to fling both my arms around his neck, but resisted it. There was important business at hand. However, as our faces came level, his lips brushed my cheek. I offered the other one and he kissed it. We smiled at each other with satisfaction and turned to the windowpane.

The view was as I had declared last night: sky. A glorious sky to be sure, the colour of forget-me-nots and speckled with birds in full cry – but sky nevertheless. "You see?" I asked him. "This room is too high to see anything from the windows except the sky, unless you are looking downwards. And she did not point downwards."

"But she put her forehead on the glass, did she not?"

"Yes, lower down."

"So could she be showing you what she wanted you to do with the *middle* pane?"

Of course she was. She had given her instructions, but I had been too dull to understand them. "You are quite right!" I exclaimed. "I climbed up, but I didn't put my forehead on the glass!"

"Then do so now," he instructed. "Lean forward, put your forehead on the middle pane, and look downwards. I have got you; you will not fall."

I did as he asked. I could still see sky, but now I could also see the tops of the trees that lined the glen. They grew thickly among the rocks, some so ancient they resembled rocks themselves. In particular, a spreading pine appeared in the very centre of the view. "I see that pine," I said. "The big one."

"Let me look."

I moved out of the way and he placed his own forehead against the glass. His body was close enough for me to feel, rather than hear, his intake of breath. "Good God, Cat, that's it!" He raised his head and looked at me with elation. "It is not the tree. It is what is *beneath* it." He let go of my waist, got off the chair and leaned against the window frame. "There is another cave, down there in the glen. MacGregor never tires of pointing out the place where the land slid and an old oak fell across the entrance. It is directly beneath that pine tree!"

I was still standing on the chair. In his excitement, he grasped me around my knees. "We must go down there today – immediately!"

Almost overbalancing, I steadied myself by putting my

hands on his shoulders and he lifted me down. "Jamie," I began warily, "be sensible. The cave, as you have just told me, is blocked by an old tree. We cannot get in, even if the ghost wishes us to."

He stood back and contemplated me with affection. "Darling Cat, that is exactly why we have to go and investigate. Do you not see? The cave has been inaccessible for twenty years. But those twenty years were before *you* came. Now you are here, this girl is telling us something about the cave, accessible or not. We cannot admit defeat until we have seen what is down there with our own eyes."

My spirits sank. "Is it dangerous?" I dreaded the thought of a visit to another cave. "Your grandmother says—"

"My grandmother hates all the caves and thinks they should be bricked up. But they are not dangerous. You have seen that yourself."

I was not so sure. When Jamie had left me alone in the caves, I had been assailed by panic. There might not have been any actual danger, but the sensation of being lost, blind and helpless was not one I wished to repeat. "Why do you not go alone?" I suggested.

"Because the ghost has indicated the place to *you*!" He could not disguise his exasperation, though he still gazed at me kindly. "She is your guide and you must be mine!"

I sat down on the chair, defeated. It was futile to argue, or try to refute him with logic; we were in the grip of something that defied logical explanation.

"You cannot go alone," said Jamie. He was standing in front of the window, his face silhouetted by the daylight; I could not see his expression. But I heard earnestness in his voice. "I am not so much of a coward that I would allow it. But you must come, do you see?"

I did see. I pondered for a moment, struck by a sudden memory. My father, whose best friend had been a soldier, used to say, "All soldiers are frightened as they ride into battle, but not one amongst them is cowardly." I was frightened, but if Jamie was not a coward, then neither was I.

"Very well, then," I told him. "I suppose now the ghost has brought me this far, I had better go the rest of the way."

He grinned. "That's my Cat! You are as curious as any other cat, are you not?"

"I suppose I am." Apprehensively, I tried to return his smile. "But I am not as agile. I do not always fall on my feet."

"Why are you wearing that dress?"

Jamie was looking at me critically, shading his eyes against the sun. The light was so relentless it had turned the side of the glen into a glittering wall, blackening the shadows so completely that I did not know how we were going to find the right tree. "Because it is the one I put on this morning," I told him blankly, looking down at the dove-coloured striped cotton that reached to my ankles, supported as usual by two petticoats. It was my thinnest dress and I had not had time to have any summer mourning

132

made. Father, I was sure, would not disapprove.

"For the love of God," sighed Jamie, "why can girls not wear sensible clothes?"

I was offended. "Like every other girl, I wish I could!"

He was standing in a shaft of sunlight. I saw his teeth glint as he smiled. "You can put on an old pair of my trousers and my smock, which needs mending anyway, and we can climb down together like mountaineers!"

I began to laugh. "I cannot dress in your clothes!"

He caught me around the waist and pulled me to him. "Why not?"

Objections failed me. "Well, if I must. But I will never get out of the house without someone seeing me. You had better bring the clothes here and I will put them on."

He scampered off, whipping the twig this way and that. I took two or three tentative steps down the glenside, but was soon stopped by a knee-high wall of bracken, immoveable against my skirt. I picked up the hem and tried to make further progress, holding the skirt up and away from my body, but it was clear: a girl in a long dress and two petticoats cannot climb down a rocky hillside. I needed my hands for balance, not for holding up my skirt.

I sat down on a stump and raised my face to the warmth of the sun. Something caught the corner of my vision. I shaded my eyes. On the other side of the glen, where the trees thinned and the grouse moor began, a kilted man leaned on a stick. It was MacGregor. I was wearing a light-coloured dress; I could not have made myself more obvious against the dark greens and browns if I had tried. I waved to him. He did not wave back, though I was certain he had seen me.

I got up and entered the shadow behind a tangle of branches, out of MacGregor's view. After a few minutes Jamie appeared with a bundle in his arms. Taking it from him, my heart turned over; the smock smelled of carbolic soap and cigarettes, like Jamie himself.

"If you were a gentleman, you would turn your back," I told him.

He grinned. "And if you were a lady, you would go behind that tree so I did not have to."

The rowan tree was in full foliage; I could not have had a better screen as I stripped off my dress, then, after a moment's hesitation, my corset as well. When I put the trousers on over my drawers it was a strange sensation. The garments were the least restricting I had ever worn; I might as well be in my nightdress. I took the black ribbon from the crown of my head and used it to tie all my hair back, as I had worn it when I was twelve. Now, resembling something between a man and a woman, a child and an adult, I emerged from behind the rowan tree.

"Do you approve?" I asked Jamie.

He spun round and burst into laughter. "You look even more ridiculous than before!"

"Thank you."

"But as lovely as ever," he added, still chuckling. Then, serious again, he took my hand. "Now, tread where I tread, and hold onto anything you can with your other hand. I know what the climb is like. I used to roam all over this glen as a boy."

We began our descent of the steep slope among tangled trees and shrubs. My boots encountered scrubby patches of grass, spongy moss, rotted leaves, tree roots and muddy ridges. Even though I was following in Jamie's footsteps, I misjudged my footing several times and slid down the glenside help-lessly for a few inches, sometimes more. If he had not clasped my hand tightly, I would have fallen. But I did not complain. The daring feeling of being without my corset and petticoats in the daytime, and the sheer elation of being with Jamie, drove me on.

"This must be the one." He had stopped and was leaning breathlessly against the broad trunk of a pine tree, so tall that its green–black mass obliterated the sky. We stood in the gloom, our feet sinking into the mulch of pine needles around the trunk. "Huzzah!" he concluded in triumph.

The tree stood on an earthy but solid-looking ledge. I stepped carefully to the edge and peeped over. I saw noth-ing but more trees, stretching downwards in a solid mass, all the way to the bottom of the glen. "I understood," I began gently, not wishing to deflate him, "that the blocked cave is underneath this tree."

"It is." He was still smiling, but his eyes questioned me.

"Jamie, there is nothing here but more trees."

His face straightened in discontent. He pushed himself off the trunk and came to the edge. "It *is* there," he insisted, peering down the glenside. "MacGregor says so!"

I looked around, unsure whether to feel disappointed or relieved. "Could he have been mistaken? Or perhaps this is not the right tree after all."

At that moment we heard the sound of someone climbing up the slope. I turned to see MacGregor's tam-o'-shanter bobbing between the tree trunks. He had crossed the valley and was making his way towards us, pulling himself up with his stick and grunting with the effort. When he reached the pine tree he stopped, gave me an inscrutable look and turned to Jamie. "Mr Jamie, sir, a message from your father. Will ye go back to the house as soon as ye can?"

"Why? What has happened?"

"I dinna ken, sir. He says for yersel' and the young lady to go back, if ye please."

I could see Jamie was not satisfied with this, but he did not challenge MacGregor's words. "How did you know where we were, MacGregor?" he asked.

The gillie remained inscrutable, deliberately not looking at me in my strange garb. "I saw ye's from the hill. Miss Graham waved to me. I got on with my work, then a wee while later Bridie came out the house and called to me that Master wants ye back."

"Well, now you're here," said Jamie, in no hurry to obey

his father's request, "you can be of help. Miss Graham and I are looking for the entrance to the cave where the tree fell across. Is it near here?"

MacGregor's expression changed. When he spoke, his face was grimmer and his voice gruffer. "It is indeed, no more than a few yards away, down there." He pointed with his stick, further down the hillside. "Ye may see the roots of this pine tree below the ledge, that were exposed when the land slid away and the great oak fell."

So Jamie was right; the pine tree *did* show the way to the cave. I looked at him, but he was still looking at the gillie. "Have you been down there, MacGregor?" he asked sternly.

"Aye, sir."

"So it is not as dangerous as Mrs McAllister thinks?"

MacGregor's face closed up again. "It is dangerous for young persons to go clambering about there."

"Have you been into the cave yourself?" asked Jamie.

"No, sir. The tree canna be moved by beast nor man."

I was relieved. Jamie and I had obeyed the instruction of the ghostly visitor by finding the tree she had pointed out. But it looked as if I would be spared the ordeal of a visit to the inside of the cave. MacGregor waited in case Jamie had anything else to add, then he said, "Now, sir, will ye come back up to the house, as the master asks?"

Jamie nodded, and with a questioning glance at me, took hold of my hand. Together we followed MacGregor back up the glen to the spot where I had left my clothes.

"You go on," I said to Jamie. "I will follow when I am dressed."

When they were out of sight I changed, but I decided to retain at least one form of freedom: I let my hair down around my shoulders. Then I bundled the trousers and smock, and made my way between the gorse bushes to the bridge that led to the garden.

The sun was almost overhead now, bleaching the castle stone and outlining the base of the building with a narrow strip of shadow. I stepped onto the bridge, conscious that my legs were weary and I was ready for my luncheon. But halfway across, I stopped, and put the bundle of clothes behind my back. MacGregor was nowhere to be seen, but Mrs McAllister, Doctor Hamish and Jamie stood in a little knot outside the front door. The doctor looked on while Mrs McAllister, wearing her plumed hat, carried on an animated conversation with Jamie. Even from a distance, I could tell that she was scolding him, and as I came nearer, I heard her.

"You thoughtless boy! Do you ever think of anyone but yourself?" Without pausing for him to speak, she answered her own question. "No, of course you do not. Go upstairs and get ready this minute, and be quick about it!"

Her gaze fell on me as I approached. "And as for you" – she narrowed her eyes against the sunlight and scrutinized me – "that dress is too thin and you must put up your hair. You cannot go to town looking like a farmer's daughter."

When she saw my blank expression, she turned impatiently to her son-in-law. "Hamish! Have you not told Catriona of our plans? You are as forgetful as your son!"

The doctor made a gesture of apology. "It is regrettable, Jean, that today's outing has been delayed, but it is no matter. I asked Jamie to be ready for an early luncheon, and to tell Catriona, as she had gone to bed and I knew I would be leaving before breakfast. Clearly, it slipped his mind." His eyes flicked to Jamie. "Do as your grandmother says, and put on your good suit. We must finish quickly – we are awaited at one o'clock."

As Jamie passed behind me, he relieved me of the bundle of clothes. Doctor Hamish saw, but made no comment about it, addressing me in his usual kind way. "Let me enlighten you, my dear. I am concerned that you might be rather bored with day-to-day life here at the castle, so I have arranged an excursion to the surgery, and to Drumwithie itself. I thought it might be interesting for you to visit our wee town, though of course it is hardly a town at all, compared to Gilchester."

I was touched. "I am not at all bored, but how considerate you are!"

"MacGregor has orders to bring the trap round," continued the doctor, "but I shall ride down on Jennie, so that I may see my afternoon patients as usual and ride back up for supper."

"Thank you very much," I said warmly, hoping the words conveyed my true appreciation of the invitation.

"It is our pleasure." He slid a glance at Mrs McAllister. "Is it not, Jean?"

She gave an unsmiling nod. "Your hair, Catriona?" she reminded me. "Luncheon is waiting."

I ran into the Great Hall, and down the kitchen corridor, all the while calling, "Bridie! Bridie!"

Bridie came out of the kitchen door, smoothing her apron, her face expectant. "Aye, miss?"

"Have you a moment to come up and do my hair?" I asked. "We are going out and I am not tidy. Did you brush my skirt?"

She was as eager to help me as I was to have her help. Quickly, she took the roast chicken off the spit and set it on a platter to keep warm by the fire. "I'll be with ye as soon as I can change my apron, miss."

It turned out that Bridie was practised with the brush and pins. She told me she had two younger sisters, whose hair she had often attended to when they were all girls at home. When she had finished, the tangle of strands had been smoothed into a neat roll, pinned on top, and set off by the elegant placing of my grandmother's mother-of-pearl comb. Bridie made no comment, of course, but when I put on my cleaned, pressed skirt and stood before the mirror, I saw her behind me, pink-faced with pride.

"Thank you, Bridie."

She dropped a miniscule curtsey, her flush deepening.

"And now I must rush," I said. "They are waiting for me."

In fact, they were waiting for Jamie. When he appeared, in a grey suit, with a bowler hat in his hand, I tried not to gasp; I had never seen him look so formal, or so normal. But as we took our places, the old Jamie returned. "Hrrmph!" he exclaimed. "I hope Bridie has cooked a horse, because I could eat one! And I would wager Cat could too. We have wandered all over the valley this morning."

"Jamie Buchanan, all you think about is food," said Mrs McAllister, though not disagreeably.

"Not true!" protested Jamie. "I have been known to think of poetry, for instance. And even, sometimes, young ladies."

It was impossible not to smile. I did not look at Jamie's grandmother, but I was sure she was looking at me curiously. Under the table, Jamie's fingers enclosed mine. Perhaps she saw that too. "Be quiet and make haste," she scolded. "We must not be late at the surgery."

The necessity of eating quickly silenced us all. After luncheon, when Doctor Hamish had departed on his horse, I collected my hat and parasol, and Jamie donned his bowler. It made him look unnatural, like a boy dressed as a man. I suppressed the urge to laugh.

"Did you enjoy your climb up the glen this morning, MacGregor?" he asked as he handed his grandmother into the trap. "It is a fine day for it, is it not?"

MacGregor did not turn round from the driving seat. "Aye, sir."

Mrs McAllister and I put up our parasols, though we

scarcely needed them, so short and shady was the journey downhill. But a lady without a parasol on a sunny day was not an acceptable sight, and had not been so for a hundred years. Perhaps, I reflected, we would still be carrying them in a hundred years' time, when, as my father had confidently predicted, people would be travelling around the world in flying machines.

The trap drew up outside a low stone house. It had the small windows and slate roof of most of the other houses in Drumwithie, but instead of opening straight off the street, it had a courtyard surrounded by a low wall, with a well-swept path to the polished door. Inscribed on a brass plaque beside the gate were the words *Dr H. G. Buchanan, M.D.* A notice in one of the glass door panels read, *Surgery hours, morning 8 to 12 o'clock, afternoon 2 to 5 o'clock. Closed Saturday afternoons. Please ring the bell and enter.*

So this was where Doctor Hamish worked. My seat in the trap afforded me a good view of my surroundings. Further along the street was a row of shops and a church, and down the hill, away from the older part of the village, I could see the gate to the station. Drumwithie was, as the doctor had intimated, a small town, not picturesque, but with an air of timelessness and peace.

Jamie helped his grandmother and me down from the trap. We stood on the sunlit cobbles while MacGregor set Kelpie clip-clopping towards the public house on the corner.

"That man had better not take more whisky than is good

for him," observed Mrs McAllister. "The track up to the castle is narrow."

"*I* can drive us, Grandmother," Jamie reassured her. "And anyway, you know MacGregor only gets drunk on Saturday nights."

"Do not use that vile expression, Jamie!" she exclaimed as he opened the front door for her. "If you must describe the condition, the word is *intoxicated*."

Two doors led off the simple hallway, one marked *Waiting Room* and the other *Surgery*. From the waiting room emerged a woman in a white apron and nurse's cap. She was small and thin, and about Mrs McAllister's age. "It'll be a fine day ye've brought with ye's!" she said good-naturedly.

"Good day, Spencer," said Mrs McAllister. "This is Miss Graham, Doctor Hamish's relation from England, who is spending the summer with us."

Spencer looked at me admiringly. "Aye, I've heard all about the lassie. Drumwithie is a braw grand place, is it not, Miss Graham?"

I could not help but feel self-conscious. What had Doctor Hamish been saying? But I had learnt that "braw" meant broad or large, and by association, good. "Yes, very braw," I said shyly.

Jamie laughed. "We'll make a Scot of you yet! May we go in, Spencer?" he asked the nurse, indicating the surgery door.

"Aye, Mr Jamie, the surgery is closed until two o'clock."

Spencer knocked, listened, and opened the door. "Here they are, Doctor."

"Behold!" cried Jamie, striding in. "The lion in his lair!"

Doctor Hamish rose from his seat at a mahogany desk. His "lair" was a small but well-appointed consulting room, with an examining couch, a sink with polished brass taps and cabinets full of bottles and bandages. The air, like that in every doctor's room I had ever entered, smelled of alcohol rub and floor cleaner. "Yes," he said, smiling at me, "this is where I spend my days."

"And where he would incarcerate *me*!" Jamie waited for his grandmother and me to sit down in the patients' chairs, then he perched on the edge of the couch. "Can you honestly see me here, Cat, dealing with boils and ulcers and hypochondriacs?"

"Jamie!" It was Mrs McAllister. "Do not start. Catriona does not wish to hear your grievances."

"She already knows them!" retorted Jamie.

His grandmother was struck by this. She regarded me stiffly. "So he has been telling you more than folk tales?"

I glanced nervously at Jamie, who shrugged. "He has told me of his reluctance to study medicine," I told Mrs McAllister. "We have talked about education in general."

I hoped that would be the end of it, but Mrs McAllister pursued her point. "And what is your opinion?" she asked sharply. "Should Jamie become a doctor, or follow this ridiculous notion of being a poet?"

144

Doctor Hamish came round the desk. "If you please, Jean, may we leave this subject for another occasion? Catriona has come here to be shown the surgery." He offered me his arm. "Now, my dear, I will show you where the *real* work is done."

He took me through a side door to a large, light room. Its high ceiling showed that it had been more recently constructed than the rest of the house. In the centre was a scrubbed table, and steel trays of surgical instruments waited on trolleys, half-covered with clean cloths. Doctor Hamish was evidently rather more than a country doctor.

"I had no idea you were a surgeon!" I exclaimed. "How wonderful for the people of Drumwithie, to have a hospital on their doorstep!"

The doctor smiled delightedly, his face pink above his whiskers. "I am only able to perform minor operations here, of course. But I am, if I may say so, ahead of many doctors in obstetrics. Childbirth, that is. In this room I have brought several babies into the world by Caesarian operation, and helped women through complicated labours. Without doubt, lives have been saved."

I was so impressed, I was silenced. But Jamie, who had appeared in the open doorway, spoke for me. "Father, tell Cat about the paper you wrote in that medical journal, about the reduction in the infant mortality rate of Lothian since this little cottage hospital was established? And about the medal you've got from the Royal College of Surgeons of Edinburgh?"

Doctor Hamish looked modestly at the floor. "The medical profession is endlessly striving to improve, as I'm sure you understand, Catriona," he said. "I am merely doing my bit."

"Hrrmph!" said Jamie, and turned back to the doctor's room. I looked at his father, expecting to see impatience in his eyes. But there was something else there. In a flash, I realized what it was. Jamie's melodramatic refusal to follow him into medicine was only partly born of a desire to be a poet. There was a greater, and more painful, reason for his contempt: if he could not be an even more pioneering doctor than his father, better respected by his colleagues and better loved by his patients, he would rather not enter the profession at all.

I approached the doctor. "May I say that I wish with all my heart that my dear father were here to see this? Mother, I'm sure, will be very impressed when I tell her about it. I am so grateful to you for bringing me here, and showing me your work. It is inspirational." Inspirational to everyone, I told myself silently, except the one person who had allowed the arrangements for this visit to "slip his mind" because he did not want to come.

"Thank you, my dear," said the doctor warmly. "It was, I confess, a large part of my desire to bring you to Drumwithie. David and I are cut from the same cloth, you see. In our youth, our discussions of our plans and ambitions were endless. We differed in some ways – our opinions about female education spring to mind – but we are – were – both men of action."

I remembered Mr Groves, the factory foreman, hollow-eyed beside my father's grave. Father had built his factory on progressive lines and his staff was as loyal to him as I could see that the population of Drumwithie was to his cousin. "Indeed," I agreed. "You have both achieved great things."

Jamie flung open the door and we said our goodbyes. Outside, he suddenly stood very still, intent upon my face. "I have just noticed how very *elegant* you look, Cat!"

Mrs McAllister had the decency not to comment on my discomfort. "The way you rattle on will be the ruin of you, my boy!" she warned Jamie. "Come along, no dawdling. I have errands." But as Jamie fell into step behind us, she murmured to me, "You do look nice, Catriona. And so you should. Jamie is forever at odds with me about this, but I will not have him, or anyone in a party from Drumwithie, appear in the village less than smartly dressed. It is not seemly for one in his position. People must know their place."

"Bridie dressed my hair and brushed my skirt," I said.

Mrs McAllister nodded with satisfaction. "I am glad to hear it. She needs more to do; she is getting stout. Now, I wish to make some purchases at Campbell's, and perhaps you do too?"

"Haberdashers," explained Jamie.

"Do you need any ribbons, my dear?" asked Mrs McAllister. "Or sewing thread? And …" – she lowered her voice once more – "Mrs Campbell also keeps a small selection of stockings."

I was aware that Jamie, hidden from Mrs McAllister by my parasol, was shaking his head. "Thank you, but no," I said. "I do not need anything."

"Cat and I will wait for you, Grandmother," he declared, "by the river, in that spot with the view of the church."

He led me down a cobbled slope between cottages, to a wooden seat in the shade of a stone bridge that spanned the river. It was the same river, I realized, that ran at the bottom of Drumwithie glen. That morning, Jamie and I had stood above it on the rocky ledge that supported the pine tree. The tall tree, standing proud of the others, visible from the middle pane of the tower window. My ghost's tree.

I sat down, and Jamie leaned against the arch of the bridge and lit a cigarette. "Good God, I'm glad to get away from my grandmother!" he sighed. "I can't draw breath without her criticizing me, and now she's started on *you.*" He gave me a sympathetic look. "It makes me even more relieved than I usually am that I was born male. Does your mother behave like she does?"

"Not quite, no. But she does insist on decorum."

"Ah, our trusty friend, decorum!" Sitting down beside me, he stuck his cigarette in his mouth and took off his hat and jacket. The heat of the day had smeared his hair across his brow, and the starch in his shirt collar was wilting, but he looked more beautiful than ever. My heart quivered uncertainly, but I had discovered a truth: beauty, commonly believed to be in the eye of the beholder, is in the soul of the beloved. He was beautiful because he cared for me, as I cared for him.

I cradled the thought inside me. This desire for Jamie was not a mere schoolgirl infatuation. It was meant to be. I had always been destined to come to Drumwithie, and love this strange, difficult man, full of such joy and such woe. And if I believed this, I must also believe that I really was the Cait Sìth, who had unknowingly awoken the ghost, and might yet discover how and why such a young girl had died.

There on that quiet riverbank, sleepy in the sunshine, death seemed impossible. The water flowed, the trees were bright with new leaves, the sky reached to a blue infinity. Amidst all the splendour in the world, cruel fate had taken my father away and laid him in a wooden box in St Stephen's churchyard. The memory of the box, with its brass handles, hurtled into my mind, but I squashed it. Father's body was in that box, but his spirit was here among the trees and in my heart.

I sat there, dreaming, only half-listening to Jamie's idle talk while the smoke from his cigarette disappeared into the sunlight. But the dream brought guilt as well as pleasure. How could it be that, only a few weeks after the death of my beloved father, I was happier than I had ever been?

1903

Seven years previously

*T*he boy's golden head was bent over his porridge bowl. As usual, he was eating as ravenously as if he had not tasted food for days. At fourteen years old, he was growing quickly.

"Shall I ask Bridie for more toast?" she suggested, seeing there were only two slices left in the rack. Her husband, late for the surgery, had hurried out, a slice in each hand, to the stable.

The boy's mouth was full, so he shook his head instead of trying to speak. She was pleased to see it; her decision to continue to educate him at home instead of sending him to school was paying off. His manners were daily becoming more gentlemanly. His father had reported that the execution of his schoolwork was improving too, and had shown her some recent work selected by his tutor. She had been particularly taken by the accuracy and neatness of his map-drawing.

She poured herself a second cup of tea. "Do you have geography today?" she asked him. "I thought your map of Canada and the United States was extremely well done."

He was scraping up the last of his porridge onto his spoon. "I like

150

drawing," he told her, "but I don't like geography much. Today I have Latin verbs to learn, then French with Monsieur Lavelle this afternoon."

She nodded, glancing at the clock. "Well, if you are finished with your breakfast, you had better get to your books."

He kissed her cheek and left the dining room. She heard his boots striking the flagstones, then thudding on the library carpet. Why could fourteen-year-old boys not walk quietly?

Bridie came in to clear the table before the second cup of tea was drunk. "Oh, Bridie, we seem to be running a little late this morning," she said. "Will you sit down and we can go through the list here, to save time?"

"Aye, madam, I have it in my apron pocket."

Wednesday was shopping-list day. Bridie took the list from her pocket and sat in the boy's place. Familiarity with servants was greater at Drumwithie than it had been at her father's vicarage, but even here it would have been unthinkable for Bridie to sit in the master's chair. They pored over the list together. All the usual things were there. She granted Bridie's request for two packets of laundry starch instead of one, and the task was finished.

"I'll be away to the kitchen, then, madam," said Bridie. "Baking today, ye ken."

"Oh, yes!" She handed Bridie her empty cup. "May we have scones? Jamie loves them so, and he seems to need so much food these days!"

"Aye, no bother, madam. There's plenty of sour milk to use up."

"Thank you, Bridie."

Drawing her shawl about her shoulders, she went through the

boot room and out of the side door. She had to pick up the hem of her dress as she made her way across the dew-soaked grass and into the scrubbier vegetation of the glenside. Once she had entered the caves and was standing in the first chamber, she let her skirts go. They swept the damp floor as she felt her way along the wall to the next cave, and up the staircase to the one with the slit between the boulders.

The stripe of daylight bisected the gloom. She could just see the place where the passageway led off the cave, and when she went towards it, she could hear the water splashing into the pool.

Quickly, she took off her shawl and jewellery. She left her wedding ring and the tortoiseshell comb her husband had given her on their tenth anniversary in the centre of the folded shawl. Then she slipped off her house shoes. Her stockinged feet silent on the wet stone, she felt her way along the wall towards the sound of the trickling water, and the promise of oblivion.

THE SILVER CASE

Meals at Drumwithie Castle followed rituals as predict-
able as train timetables. At suppertime, we did not
change our clothes, but went straight to the dining room.
Water, never wine, was served at table. The doctor would
sometimes pour himself a whisky from the cupboard in the
corner of the Great Hall, and drink it with his after-supper
coffee. But he never offered Jamie or me a "dram", as he
called it.

On the evening of our visit to the surgery, our early
luncheon ensured I was ready for supper. I washed sketchily,
pleased to see that Bridie's skill had kept my hair much neater
than usual. My heart was light; I took the shallow stairs
quickly, and almost stumbled through the open door of the
dining room.

Bridie was alone there, putting the finishing touches to the
table. Wine glasses had been set out, I noticed, and there was a
bowl of roses in the centre of the cloth. The ritual, it seemed,

had been broken. "Are we expecting company?" I asked.

Bridie stood back from the table and inspected it. "Aye, miss. Mrs McAllister is here."

"But—" I began, about to protest that she had come to luncheon and *never* came to supper on the same day. But I remembered who I was speaking to. "The table looks beautiful."

"Orders are to lay a nice table when Mrs McAllister comes, miss."

"Ah." If I had known, I would have changed into my evening dress. "Thank you, Bridie. Are the others in the Great Hall?"

"Aye, miss."

I sighed, anticipating another admonishment from Jamie's grandmother. But when I entered the Great Hall, I was relieved to see that Jamie had changed into his usual comfortable clothes, and the doctor still had on the tweed jacket he wore to work. Mrs McAllister's influence on the Buchanans' preference for an informal supper was, perhaps, weaker than she might have wished.

Jamie was sprawled on a hard chair, a book in his hand, while Mrs McAllister sat at the fireside. The doctor sprang up from the other armchair and went to the corner cupboard. "Catriona, may I offer you a nip?"

Jamie laughed loudly at my surprised expression. "He is not going to pinch you! A 'nip' is Scots for a small drink." He nodded towards the bottle his father had taken from the cupboard. "In this case, sherry."

154

I sat down on the chair next to Jamie's. "I thought a small drink was a 'dram'."

"And so it is, but a dram is more often used when the drink in question is whisky," said the doctor, setting out glasses.

"That can also be a 'tot'," added Jamie. "But sherry is always a 'nip'."

Doctor Hamish was looking at me from under his eyebrows. "Does your mother allow you wine now and then, my dear?"

"I had some champagne at a wedding we went to last summer."

"And did you like it?"

"Not much. It was so fizzy, it stung the roof of my mouth."

"Hah!" exclaimed Jamie with a delighted grin. "Then you did not consume enough of it to appreciate the pleasure of its effects!"

While he and his father were laughing at this, I slid a look towards Mrs McAllister, who had remained silent. She neither laughed nor spoke, but gave an almost invisible nod.

"I will try sherry, if you please, doctor," I said.

He poured some of the golden liquid into a very small glass and handed it to me. "If I give you any more than this, my dear, we shall have to carry you to the dining room," he observed, mock-serious.

I sniffed the sherry. It had a deep, evocative scent. When the doctor said "Cheers!", I raised my glass with everyone else, and sipped. The drink was sweet, but very strong. I felt its warmth as I swallowed. I took another sip.

"So, Catriona," said Mrs McAllister, putting down her glass on a polished table, "I trust you are enjoying your stay at Drumwithie?"

"Oh, yes! Very much, thank you."

"And what do you like in particular?"

She pronounced it "part-ic-u-lar", in her precise Scottish voice. Rapidly, I sifted through memories of the last week. If I were to tell her that the guest room was haunted by the ghost of an unknown young woman, or that I myself was haunted, in a less supernatural way, by the sad beauty of Jamie's mother, what would she think of me? Under this roof I had experienced extremes of emotion I had never encountered before, from delicious happiness to fear and repulsion. But could I tell her that? Of course not.

I smoothed my skirt. "The view from the tower room is very fine," I said. "I never tire of looking at it."

Mrs McAllister raised her eyebrows. "Indeed? I would have thought a person of your tender years would prefer the more animated pleasures the country has to offer. Have you not explored the woods?"

"Er ... Jamie and I went a little way down the glenside this morning, but MacGregor came and gave us the message to come to luncheon, so—"

"Hamish!" demanded Mrs McAllister. "Why has this poor girl not been shown the woods? The *real* woods?"

The doctor, standing in his favourite spot before the fire, took a sip of his drink. "The *real* woods?"

"You know the woods of which I speak," she said in an I-have-the-measure-of-you tone. She turned back to me. "The castle grounds are magnificent, as I am quite sure you agree. But beyond them lies glorious woodland, where some of the trees are among the most ancient in Scotland. The woods are some walk away, but Hamish and my daughter did their courting there. I well remember that I wore out two pairs of very good boots before the ring was on her finger!"

I pictured Anne, doggedly shadowed by her mother, when she wished to walk alone with her future husband. "I would like very much to see the woods," I said, glancing involuntarily at Jamie.

He was staring at his father, frowning. "Grandmother speaks of Blairguthrie's woods, does she not, Father? But I thought Blairguthrie did not allow anyone on his property."

Doctor Hamish put his glass down on the mantelpiece and addressed Jamie calmly. "You were forbidden to go there as a child, because your mother was afraid of shooting parties and poachers' traps."

Mrs McAllister snorted. "Of *course* one cannot go there in the shooting season, and traps are a danger wherever you go in this part of the country," she declared impatiently. "But Blairguthrie has always allowed us to walk in his woods in the summer, as you well know!"

The doctor and his son looked at each other. In Jamie's

face I saw distrust; in his father's, unease. "Now you are grown up, Jamie," said Doctor Hamish, "you may go there if you please. But do not expect me to accompany you. I no longer wish to visit the woods."

Mrs McAllister, unwilling to be seen as the cause of conflict, and perhaps realizing that she had trespassed on her son-in-law's painful memories of a young, healthy Anne, took refuge in exaggerated astonishment. "But you must! I *insist* you take Catriona up there before the end of her stay!"

The doctor drained his glass, avoiding his mother-in-law's gaze. "Then she and Jamie may go, if they wish. They seem happy enough in each other's company. But as I have already said, I do not go there."

Mrs McAllister was not to be bested. "Then MacGregor must go with them!" she demanded. "You cannot allow two young people—"

"Jean!" Doctor Hamish felt in his pockets and withdrew a small, silver cigarette case. It was the one my mother had given him as a remembrance of my father. He took out a cigarette and lit it, his fingers fumbling slightly. "Jean, if you please, let us speak no more about it."

An unstoppable flush was creeping up my neck. Everyone seemed displeased. And I had offended Mrs McAllister. Although the impropriety of being left alone with Jamie had crossed my mind, I had dismissed it. We had been left unsupervised to fall in love. But on today's visit to town, I had been chaperoned in his presence. Even when

158

Mrs McAllister had allowed us to wander down to the river together, we had not been out of sight of the haberdasher's shop. The freedom we had enjoyed for more than a week had apparently come to an end.

Mrs McAllister opened her mouth to speak, but shut it unexpectedly, letting out a whimper. Her hand was at her throat. "Hamish, that cigarette case!" She was searching his face with troubled eyes. "David had one exactly the same, with that blue thistle on it. There cannot be two such—"

"Actually, it *is* David's," interrupted the doctor matter-of-factly, dropping the case back into his pocket. "Mrs Graham was kind enough to give it to me." He glanced at the clock. "Now, shall we go in?"

Mrs McAllister rose from her chair on a perfect perpendicular, like a marionette picked up by a puppeteer. She was at her most dignified, her deportment as immaculate as only a lifetime of expensive corsetry could produce. But beneath the brim of her hat, her eyes – as brightly sea-green, I noticed for the first time, as her grandson's – remained distracted.

Why had my father's cigarette case caused such agitation? As we went into the dining room, I stole another glance at her. All imperiousness was gone. She looked like an unhappy woman past her prime, oppressed beyond endurance, and longing only for peace.

At ten o'clock Mrs McAllister went home. But although my eyes smarted with fatigue, I found myself loath to go upstairs. I had begun to fear the darkness of the tower room. Jamie went to return his book to the library, but I stayed in my chair, my heart murmuring uneasily, while Doctor Hamish put out lights and checked the windows were closed.

When he turned and saw me there, he smiled kindly. "Let me get you a candle, my dear."

Bridie was already in her room, and MacGregor, who usually fetched the candles, had not yet returned from driving Mrs McAllister back to the Lodge. Beyond the door of the Great Hall, the house was covered in impenetrable blackness, denser than I had ever seen. The sky had clouded thickly during the evening, obliterating the moon and stars.

I thanked the doctor, gripping the arms of my chair so that he would not see my hands shaking. As he approached the door to the kitchen passageway, Jamie came back.

"Going for candles," his father informed him.

Jamie made a face behind his back. "If my illustrious father would dig his hand deep enough in his pocket, we would have no need of *candles*," he told me tartly. "Even the most ordinary house is connected to the gas supply these days!"

"But Drumwithie is no ordinary house."

He must have heard some apprehension in my voice, because he whipped round, full of concern. "What is the matter?"

I could not speak; I could hardly breathe. In a second Jamie was kneeling at my feet, taking my hands, exclaiming at how cold they were, and gazing into my face. "You are nervous. Darling Cat, is it my grandmother? Did she upset you this evening?"

I tried to shake my head, but Jamie went on, not noticing. "But you know, you need not heed her. My father is the master of Drumwithie. She is not its mistress, and neither is she your mother." He embraced me and kissed both my cheeks warmly. "If I wish to be alone with you I will, and no one can stop me."

"Jamie…" I tried to whisper in case Doctor Hamish came back, but my breath came unevenly. "It is not that. It is… I am afraid to go to bed, in case the girl comes again, or I am beset by those hideous noises. I dread the thought of another disturbed night."

"Oh, my love." He was looking at me with tenderness, frowning, trying to understand. "Don't be anxious. You are the medium through which the ghost is speaking to us. She cannot hurt you, so—"

"But she can *frighten* me!"

He was taken aback. He regarded me silently for a moment, his green eyes glittering. Then, as his father's shadow appeared on the wall, he stood up and held his hand out for mine. "Come on, I will come up with you."

We took our candles, and Doctor Hamish put out the last lamp and closed the door behind us. "I am going to light Cat to the tower, Father," announced Jamie. "That staircase is easy for a lady to stumble on, and it is very dark tonight."

"Good boy," said the doctor, starting up the main staircase. "I wish you both goodnight."

We followed slowly. I held my skirt with one hand and the candle with the other; Jamie's free arm encircled my waist. It was comforting to feel him there and know he cared for me. But however lovingly he behaved, he could not protect me from the moment when I would be left alone in that room. I had already decided I would not put out the oil lamp tonight, in the hope of discouraging spirits, or at least assuaging my fear of them. But if the girl in the ragged dress should appear, and fix me again with her pale gaze, only *I* must face her. As Jamie had declared, she would not come if anyone else was there.

When we reached the spiral staircase, which was only wide enough for one, Jamie led the way. He opened the door to the tower bedroom; the candlelight danced round it as he crossed to the table and turned on the lamp. "There," he said. "No need to fear." He smiled calmly, his face without shadows, in the full glow of the light.

"I will try not to," I told him uncertainly. "But do you remember we discussed why the vision appears only in this room, and we thought perhaps the girl had died here? Ghosts haunt the place they died, do they not? I am not sure I like sleeping in a place where someone died."

Anxiety flitted across Jamie's face, but he checked it. "But bedrooms are where people die," he said reasonably. "If we all worried about that, we would never sleep anywhere. Are you sure no one has ever died in your room at home?"

"No, of course not." I put down my candle and began to take the pins out of my hair. An unbearable weariness had come over me. All I wished for was sleep. "But my room at home is not haunted." He made to speak, but I held up my hand. "*I* am a young girl, about the age of the ghost. *I* spend every night in this bed, in this room, in this tower. I adore my view, but if she suffered and died here, it is easy to imagine the same happening to me!"

I sat down despondently on the edge of the bed, drawing my hair over one shoulder, the pins in my hand. Jamie said nothing for a few moments, then he came and kissed my forehead. "Very well. I see I cannot kiss your fear away. I will arrange for you to sleep in another bedroom for the rest of your stay."

I could not tell if he was joking. "Are you sure? But what about tonight?"

"I mean, from this minute." He thought for a moment. "Look, next to my sitting room is a room so small it is usually occupied by children. There are bars on the windows, I'm afraid. The bed is not made up, but if you bring your pillows, I will get blankets from my room."

I was so grateful that my eyes filled. "Thank you," I whispered, wondering when a child had last stayed at Drumwithie. Or, for that matter, when an adult guest had last slept in the tower. No one ever seemed to call, or invite the Buchanans anywhere. They lived at Drumwithie in all its splendour, as

163

isolated as the castle itself. What had such a life been like for Anne Buchanan, the daughter of a clergyman, used to a busy parish and the comings and goings of a vicarage?

Jamie picked up his candle. "I will leave you to collect whatever you need. Come down when you are ready, and I will show you the room."

"What will we tell your father?" I asked, swallowing. "And Bridie?"

"Goodness, how you worry! I'll think of something by the morning. Now, there will be no fire in the little room, so wrap yourself up well."

When he had gone and I could no longer see the light from the candle flickering under the door, something compelled me to look at the ceiling. There were the beams: one, two, three, four. It was a pity wishes only came true if the beams were counted on the first night, because now I had something important to wish for: I longed for Jamie to find happiness, and for us to be together always.

I stood up, fighting the desire for sleep, my head full of plans. I would need my thicker nightdress, which was in my trunk. I dragged it from the corner, and it was when I opened the lid that my senses sharpened. The air around me became stifling. Out of the shadows, surrounded by a glittering haze like sun through mist, stepped the girl in the ragged dress.

Jamie was awake, I knew, only a few yards away downstairs. If I screamed he would hear me and rush upstairs, and the ghost would disappear. I took a breath, but the scream did not come. I was transfixed by her dark-eyed gaze.

"What do you want?" I blurted. "We have done your bidding. We found the tree. Now, I beg you, go back wherever you came from, and let me be!"

Still she stared at me, the pallor of her skin luminous in the aura surrounding her. "Why have you come back?" I asked, searching my memory for an explanation. "We found where the cave is. Is it something to do with the cave?"

Her head drooped, then slowly rose again. I interpreted this as affirmation. "But we cannot get in," I told her. "There is a great oak across the entrance."

This time her head turned one way, then the other. Her profile, which she had never shown me before, was very beautiful. As I looked at it, I was struck by a strong sense of recognition. The ghost girl bore a resemblance to some other, real girl I had seen quite recently. Shocked to the point of collapse, I sat down quickly on the bed. "Who are you?" I demanded. "Tell me who you are!"

She turned her head, this way and that, again. She was saying "no", but whether to my comment about the impossibility of entering the cave, or my request to know her identity, it was unclear. I watched, riveted. And I realized that I was no longer frightened of her. "Please," I told her gently. "I only wish to help you."

She went towards the window. Just as she had done before, she pointed to the middle pane. And just as before, she turned to me with a beseeching gaze. Her head inclined towards my travelling trunk with its open lid, then back to my face with an even more dramatic expression of pleading. With amazement I realized she was asking me to close the trunk. She was asking me not to leave the tower room.

I tried to speak, but the air cleared suddenly, and the vision faded away to nothing. I got up and stood in the spot where she had been. The middle pane. The tree. She was telling me that it was the right tree, and that whatever was troubling her had something to do with the cave. I went to my trunk and shut the lid. Then I tiptoed down the spiral staircase. The door next to Jamie's was open. "Jamie!" I hissed. "Jamie! Are you there?"

His head came round the door. "Where are your pillows?"

"I do not need them. She came again!"

"Oh!" He stared at me in disbelief, his arms full of blankets. "Sshh! Your father will hear!"

He drew me into the sitting room, shut the door and threw the blankets onto a chair. "What happened?"

I recounted how the ghost had looked, how she had indicated that our conclusions about the tree and the cave were correct, and had showed me I could not leave the tower. "And most astonishing, Jamie," I added, "I am no longer frightened of her."

"You see?" His face lit up with relief. "She *needs* you, so why should she harm you?" As he spoke, he began to walk about the room in an untidy circle. "This is the ghost's third

166

visitation," he said. "We do not know if that has any significance, but this latest appearance had a clear purpose. She had
to make you stay in the tower room, because her mission is
not completed. She will visit you again and again until we
find out what she wants." He stopped pacing and looked
directly at me. His hair had fallen over his eyes, and he tossed
it back impatiently. "And we can only find out what she
wants, my darling, by getting into that cave!"

That night my dreams were vivid.

I found myself in my nightdress in the tower room, but it
was not the bedroom I knew. It had been transformed into a
cold place, the same odd shape as the real tower, but with
stone walls and floor like a dungeon, and no furniture. The
windows looked out in two directions, but they were not my
windows. They were slits, made by placing two boulders so
that they almost touched, but leaving just enough space for a
shaft of light to pierce the blackness of the tower. Or perhaps
it was not a tower or a dungeon at all, but a cave?

The darkness in my dream was so thick it was palpable; I
had to part it like curtains in order to see what lay beyond it.
When I did, my eyes were assailed by a silver light, and my
ears by a silver sound. I saw an insubstantial world, full of
radiance, yet as two-dimensional as the painting of Ophelia
lying in the stream.

Visions quivered on the edges of the scene. I saw the
woman in the pool, her hair submerged, her skin gleaming

white against the black of the rock. I saw Jane Eyre frantically stamping on the bed curtains to put out the fire started by the madwoman. Crowds of crows appeared, so many that the sight filled my ears, and their cries filled my mouth, mixing up my senses with greedy glee. I know I screamed – I tasted the scream on my tongue. And then she emerged, her youth and beauty glowing, undiminished by her dirty appearance, or by my fear. I did *not* fear her, even in a dream.

The walls closed in. The tower, or the dungeon, or cave, whatever it was, changed back into solid darkness and the girl disappeared. I was blind and suffocating. I reached out my hands in case I stumbled, but they found only wet, mossy walls. Someone was speaking. "She did not die, though, did she?" Then someone else was shouting. "You can stay here for ever, for all I care!" The voices became louder. I shouted too, something incoherent, but was powerless to stop them. Eventually, when in my dream world I was on the edge of exhaustion, the terrible sound of the screaming woman came back. Despair, agony, loss – I could hear, see, taste, touch, smell everything contained in her cry. Compassion rushed through me. What had happened to her? Who was she and why, sleeping and waking, did she invade my peace?

Real exhaustion overtook me. I must have fallen into a very heavy slumber, because when I opened my eyes the clock read twenty past nine. I was surprised it was so late; the room seemed too dark, as if the dawn were still about to break. I was

168

hungry, but breakfast would have been cleared away by now.

I stretched, pushed back the covers and padded to the window. When I parted the curtains I gasped. My view had disappeared behind a wall of mist, and rain sluiced against the window pane. I had never seen clouds swirl around a high place like Drumwithie, or felt their presence so close outside the window. In Gilchester, clouds were white or grey, and stayed in the sky. They did not come down to earth and surround me, thick as candy floss, obliterating the world so completely I felt as if the tower *were* the world.

I watched with awe this new version of the familiar view, marvelling at the intensity of the downpour. Perhaps the reason no one had wakened me was simple: on a day like today, the best place to be was in bed. As I dressed, I wondered what a day when going outdoors was impossible would bring. The castle was at its most castle-like in the gloom, and unless Bridie lit every lamp in the place, it would remain so. We would be imprisoned in the semi-dark all day, or perhaps longer if the weather set in.

I stood before the looking-glass to brush my hair. My face had changed. Hours spent in the sunshine had reddened my nose and freckled my cheeks. The breeze that whipped the pine trees had also whipped my skin to a glow. Washing my hair in Scotland's famously soft water had made it shine with health, and it had grown unruly too, as I rarely tied it up any more. Drumwithie had turned me into a sunburned hobble-dehoy, prepared to put on men's trousers, drink coffee and sherry, and abandon my gloves and stockings. I looked like what Mother referred to as a "bohemian", the sort of girl who would smoke, and live with an artist in a studio in Paris, posing naked for him.

I would not do anything like that, of course, but at Drumwithie I had encountered the world of women who *would*. The poets and painters Jamie had introduced me to loved women who let their hair down and left off their stays, who suffered the infidelity of their lovers and, I imagined, met tragic ends. Did the model who had posed for *Ophelia* not catch pneumonia after lying for so long in Millais's cold bath? Or was that only a story?

Some of these women were poets themselves. Some were the sisters of poets and painters, and all were educated to a high level. I could never be like them: confident, striding through a man's world, sure of their talent and influence. The only poet I knew, as yet unpublished, of course, would be the only one I would ever meet.

These thoughts drifted round and round while I brushed my hair. "I will not be jealous of them. I will *not!*" I said to the mirror. In a flurry, I gathered my shoes and stockings in one hand, intending to put them on downstairs, thrust the shawl Mother had sent me around my shoulders, and started purposefully down the spiral staircase. In the darkness at the bottom, I almost collided with someone.

"There you are at last!" It was Jamie. "I thought you were never going to wake up!"

"I had very strange dreams." While I spoke I pulled the shawl around my shoulders and thrust my feet into my house shoes. "What terrible weather!"

"Hrrmph! There will be no cave-hunting or walking in the woods today!" He fell into step with me along the landing, taking my arm. "Good God, my father was odd about those woods, was he not? Even if he *did* court my mother there, that is hardly the fault of the woods. And the stupid thing is" – he gave me a sheepish look – "I used to go there all the time! When my father was at the surgery and my mother was in her room, my afternoons were free. I hardly ever had other boys to play with, so what else could I do but explore? Old Blairguthrie's gillie used to try and chase me off sometimes, but he was about ninety."

A thought struck me. "Is it odd too," I suggested, "that your father has never before discussed his dislike of Blairguthrie's woods with your grandmother? In twenty-one years?"

He stopped and looked at me. Something had evidently occurred to him too. His grip on my arm tightened and he took hold of my other arm as well. "You are quite right!" he exclaimed. "Just as I said, it has begun! *You* have made it happen! And now I *will* find the answer!"

"The answer to what?" I was baffled. "Not everything can be my responsibility, you know."

He let go of my arms and thrust his hands in his pockets. "The answer to these unending questions of mine. Why do I feel so ... *discontented?* No, that is not the right word. *Unsettled?*"

171

"Do you mean…" I began uncertainly, "because of your disagreement with your father?"

"No, not exactly." Concentration narrowed his eyes as he searched for words. "It is more the feeling that something is wrong, here at the castle. Something has always been wrong."

"I do not understand," I confessed.

He sighed. When he spoke his voice held a mixture of bitterness and dismay. "Oh, Cat, I love Drumwithie very much, with the part of my heart that is left over from loving those who love me. But can you imagine what it has been like to grow up here?"

I could, and it broke my heart. A boy alone, cared for by a servant, only able to be with his adored mother when her nervous illness permitted. A strong, clever, artistic boy, who should have been at school with other boys, roughing and tumbling, bringing friends home for the holidays. Jamie had been indulged yet disciplined, protected from the world yet exposed to distressing events within the castle. What could a young child understand about his mother's nervous collapse? How could he know why, between one day and the next, she no longer played with him in the garden they had made together? And later, on that day he had so vividly described to me, what horror had been impressed upon his fertile fourteen-year-old mind? Seven years later, the first thing he had shown me at the castle was the underground pool: the last place she had been, and the last connection he had with her.

"I think so," I told him gently.

"What has happened to Mother and my fear that I will have to become a doctor against my will, or lose both my father's regard and Drumwithie itself, is a burden. All my life, I have felt that whatever I do, I have never been worthy of his love, or my mother's. I am for ever at odds with the life I have been given."

I was beginning to understand. Jamie was a naturally good-humoured young man, quick to joke, full of enthusiasm, and interested in any subject that came to hand. But he was also given to dark moments, when his face lost its joy and he did or said unkind things. If he considered himself never to have met either of his parents' expectations, and feared the future, who could be surprised at these sudden glimpses of hidden unhappiness?

It was cold on the landing. I drew my shawl closer around my body, contemplating Jamie, wondering how to reply. As I did so, an imploring look came into his eyes.

"Please, my darling," he said gently, "however far-fetched this sounds, I believe us to be on the brink of discovering something that will explain why I feel as I do."

I breathed carefully, trying not to shiver. "The thing the Cait Sìth has been sent to find?"

He nodded. The imploring look had turned to sadness. "You are my only hope." He took his hands from his pockets and held them out to me. I took them and nestled close to him. "Do not leave me, Cat," he murmured.

"I will not." I had no thought of such practicalities as the University, or my mother. I listened to Jamie's heart beating in his chest and made my decision. "I will stay with you for ever, if you will let me."

"And will you help me find ... the answer?"

"Of course."

Releasing me, he gave a yawn, stretched his fingers and examined his nails. As unexpectedly as ever, his mood had changed. "Now, had we better not go and find a fire? You are frozen." He gazed at me for a moment, then bestowed upon me one of his warmest smiles. "Amid all this speculation, dearest, I can tell you something for absolutely certain. My grandmother will not attempt the hill in these conditions. We shall be free of her today."

PART THREE

THE TITHE

1910

Two weeks earlier

*S*he wanted her medicine. Surely it was time for the nurse to bring it? She longed for the wellbeing it brought and the sleep that followed directly. Oblivion was the only thing she desired, and the medicine the only thing that gave it to her.

The blind had been pulled over the window; it was dark. Why did the nurse not come? She could hear the usual evening noises of the hospital: doors being locked, footsteps in the corridor, the creaking wheels of the medicine trolley. Her medicine was on that trolley, in its little bottle, coming nearer. It would be here soon.

The door opened and she turned her head expectantly. But it was not the nurse with the little brown bottle and the measuring spoon. Instead, she saw Doctor Galway, and behind him, the trembling plumage of her mother's best hat.

"Good evening, Mrs Buchanan," said the doctor briskly. "You have a visitor."

Her mother seldom came, and never in the evening. She strode with her usual confidence to the bedside and kissed her daughter briefly, then stood back and took off her gloves. "If you will forgive us, Doctor Galway, I wish to speak to my daughter in private."

The doctor was about to acquiesce, but she raised her head from the pillow. "Doctor, I have not had my medicine!" she cried. "Do not leave me! They will forget to bring me my medicine!"

Doctor Galway bowed to both ladies. "I assure you, Mrs Buchanan, that nobody will forget your medicine. And I assure you, Mrs McAllister, that as soon as your visit is over, if you will just tap on the door, a nurse will come and show you out."

He took his leave and her mother sat down in the visitors' chair. "I know it is an inconvenient time, Anne, but I had to come," she began, busying herself with finding a place to put down her handbag. "There has been a development of which I feel compelled to inform you."

She was very, very tired, and her head ached unbearably. "Oh… It is not about Jamie, is it?"

The boy was a man of twenty-one now, but she still thought of him as her baby, the golden-haired darling she had kept by her side every day, until they had taken her away from Drumwithie and brought her to this place. That morning, when she had descended to the caves, intending never to ascend again, he had been going off to do his Latin with the tutor. Seven years later, he had no need for tutors. He had at last gained a place at the University. He was about to enter the world.

"Jamie is perfectly well," said her mother gently. She leaned towards the bed and took her daughter's hand. "The news, my dear, is of David."

Her heart began to thud. Blood flooded her head; silver dots floated before her eyes. "David?" she said breathlessly. A wild notion had come to her. "Oh! Has he come back?"

Her mother's head was bowed so low that only her hat feathers were visible. "No, he has not. He passed away a week ago last Monday." She stroked her daughter's hand. "He had been ill for some time, though we knew nothing of it."

She stared at her mother. "David is dead?"

"I am afraid so. Hamish read the death announcement in The Times. He has gone down to Gilchester, the town where David lived, for the funeral."

She sat up, fighting her fatigue, refusing to believe her mother's words. "Hamish has gone to David's funeral? No, you must be mistaken."

Her mother gazed at her with a look of agony. "He wished to make amends to David's family. They were cousins, after all."

She lay back again, weakened by the onslaught of many emotions, longing more than ever for her medicine. So Hamish had gone to pay his respects to David in death, when he had detested him, and severed all connection with him, in life. She did not understand her husband. She never would. What was clear, though, was that her mother had waited until Hamish was away from the castle before bringing the news. Hamish did not know of her visit, and Jamie could not know either. "Mother…" she whispered.

"Yes, my darling?" Her mother half rose, the better to hear her.

"Is it true, that David has gone?"

"Yes."

"Then there is nothing left but to join him."

Her mother sat down again, her head falling onto her breast. She had her own griefs. What comfort could she be to one who had lost everything? "Do not say that, Anne," she said softly. "Jamie is left. You must not forsake your son."

She closed her eyes. "My son." Tears slid from under her lids and down her cheeks. She felt her mother wipe them with a handkerchief. She smelled lavender on it. She remembered how this same gesture had comforted her when she was a little girl, when they lived in the vicarage, and Father was alive, and none of them had even heard of Hamish Buchanan, his cousin David Graham, or Drumwithie Castle.

Her voice rose to a wail; she could not suppress her anguish. She could not help herself screaming. Her mother's arms encircled her, but no amount of consolation could stem the grief that flooded over her, through her, soaking every crevice of her mind and body.

David was the man she had loved. He, and only he, had woken passion in her. For so many unhappy years she had carried that memory, conscious that as long as he was alive in the world, he might someday return to her. But now, even that faint hope had gone.

She screamed louder. Screams obliterated thoughts. Tears rolled into her mouth and dripped off her chin. She choked and sniffed, unthinking, aware only of the pain of her loss.

Then the feel of the arms embracing her changed from silk to scratchy tweed. Doctor Galway was restraining her, speaking in her ear, holding her head against his chest while the nurse pressed the spoon against her lips. She swallowed gratefully. It was over.

Warm among the pillows, her body, and the world, seemed insubstantial. She was calm.

From somewhere, words floated towards her ears, but she did not respond.

She did not open her eyes. She preferred the darkness. David had gone away and there was nothing left. And very soon, she would go away too, and be with him for ever.

THE SLIDE

The rain did not stop. The ground, hardened by weeks of fine weather, could not absorb the deluge, and huge puddles formed on the driveway. Water cascaded down the roof, spilling in torrents from gutters and pipes too narrow to contain its volume.

By the following day, the relentless drumming had become the background to our lives. And still it did not stop. I spent the morning in my room, writing to Mother. How I longed for her! It was scarcely credible that I had left Chester House less than two weeks ago. But the event that had so fundamentally changed my life during that short time was the very one I could not write down: Jamie and I loved each other. I wrote of the weather, our imprisonment in the castle, the delicious raspberry pudding Bridie had made, and the wonders she worked with my hair. I asked dutifully after Edith, Susan, Mrs Jamison and Jarvis. I sent my greetings to the

Reverend Baxter, and to the grocer's wife, who was lying-in after the birth of her sixth child. I even remembered to enquire after the health of Sergeant, Mother's thoroughbred, who had had a slight cough.

Then I sat back, chewing my pen. The little world of Gilchester seemed so remote, and its concerns so meaningless, I could not conjure it. In the forefront of my thoughts, as insistent as the rain streaming down my window, stood the figure in the pink silk dress, and Jamie's gleaming gaze.

I left the unfinished letter on the table. Who knew when MacGregor would be able to get to the post office, anyway? Discontented, I went downstairs.

I found the Great Hall deserted. I went to look for Jamie, but he was not in the library or the drawing room. In the passage-way to the kitchen I met Bridie. "Where is Mr Jamie?" I asked.

"Gone out, miss."

"Gone out?" I was astonished.

"Aye, he went off with MacGregor."

"When?"

"I've a mind it must have been about an hour ago, miss. I heard Mr Jamie and MacGregor speaking, and then they went out the boot-room door."

I had no wish to return to the tower room. I could not even see my precious view. All there was to do was plod on with my letter and think. "Very well," I told Bridie, "I will be in the small drawing room."

"Aye, miss," she said good-naturedly. "It's good and warm in there."

I had no sooner opened the door than boots sounded on the flagstones of the Great Hall, and Jamie appeared, followed by MacGregor. Both were thoroughly drenched. The shoulders of Jamie's overcoat were sodden, his hat dripping, and his boots and trousers heavy with wet mud. MacGregor's boots, socks and kilt hem were equally filthy. The gillie's face was pinched with anxiety.

"Cat, there's been a slide!" announced Jamie importantly. "Some of the big trees have fallen!"

I gazed at him numbly. He had taken off his hat, and was rubbing his streaming hair with his scarf. "We do not yet know which ones," he told me. "MacGregor and I tried to go down there to see, but it's impossible. We shall have to wait until the weather lets up."

His expression made it clear that he was thinking the same thing as I was: if the tree that had blocked the entrance to the cave had fallen away, the mouth of Drumwithie's underground labyrinth might once more be accessible. Dread the caves though I did, I felt a tingle of excitement.

"The master must decide what to do," declared MacGregor.

Jamie nodded. "I will speak to my father about it as soon as he returns this evening." He took off his wet things and handed them to the gillie. "Thank you, MacGregor."

When the gillie had stumped off to the boot room, Jamie

pulled me towards him and kissed me. He was warm from his exertions, rosy-cheeked, his hair darkened by its recent soaking, but beginning to dry in golden wisps. I received and returned the kiss with equal warmth, electrified by the sensation, and we kissed again and again. When we eventually drew apart, in his eyes I read a sort of discontented delight, or delightful discontent – double-edged, like many of Jamie's expressions. "You have done this!" he exclaimed.

The rain beat against the windowpanes. The wind rattled the frames. Bridie had built a good fire in the Great Hall, but I was still not warm enough and shuddered in my shawl. I wished he would take me in his arms again. "The Cait Sìth has done it, you mean?" I asked.

"Of course. If that oak tree trunk falls further down the glen, we will be able to get into the cave. Why would the ghost draw our attention to it if we could not enter it? She *knew* you would make this happen!"

Of course I had not made it rain, but I did not object. It was impossible to reason with the unreasonable. I gave a small sigh. "Will you kiss me again?"

"With pleasure!" He laughed, taking my face in his hands. But at the same moment, the door opened. Jamie let me go as suddenly as if my cheeks were red-hot. Demonstrations of affection were not permitted in front of servants, even in a liberal household like Drumwithie. But it was not only Bridie who entered. Behind her was Mrs McAllister.

"Grandmother!" Jamie raised his eyebrows in my direction

while Bridie took Mrs McAllister's mackintosh and left the room. "This is an unexpected pleasure, in this weather!"

Mrs McAllister eyed him coldly. "As if you didn't know that we Scots are made of hardy stuff! I hailed the milk van as it passed the Lodge. I can do more good here than sitting at home in my room."

I could imagine the "good" she intended to do. She was clearly aware that in such conditions, the doctor would not ride up to the house for luncheon, and Jamie and I would be left alone all day. Feeling disappointed, I warmed my hands at the fire. "Are you joining us for luncheon, Mrs McAllister?"

She sat down in the fireside chair. "I am indeed," she said steadily, studying my face. "And then, Catriona, you and I had better spend the afternoon at something useful, and leave Jamie to his studies."

During the next half-hour Mrs McAllister spoke more than I had expected. She behaved like an attentive hostess, at pains to keep the conversation flowing and superficial. She asked Jamie what he was reading. She talked of her own interest in Scottish literature, and told me, as Jamie had predicted, about the society in Edinburgh whose committee she sat on, dedicated to the preservation of folklore. When this subject was exhausted, she asked me what "useful" things I liked to do. "Do you sew, my dear?"

I had been taught to sew, but I did not care to do it, for usefulness or pleasure. "No, not really," I confessed.

"Then do you have a pony?"

"Er ... my mother is a far better horsewoman than I am. She keeps horses, but I do not have one of my own and, no, I do not often ride."

"So you do not hunt, then?"

"No."

"Ah. So what *is* your pastime, when you are at home?"

I glanced at Jamie. Intent upon the newspaper, he presented me resolutely with a view of the top of his head. "I like reading," I told his grandmother, "and sometimes I play the piano, though since Father died..."

I had not touched the piano since my father fell into his near-death sleep. When he had still been able to sit in his chair, he had liked to listen to my playing, not because I was talented – I certainly was not – but because he loved me. The music made a connection between us when other forms of discourse were no longer possible.

"Then you are musical!" said Mrs McAllister triumphantly. "I knew it! Have you brought your music with you?"

I wished I had not mentioned the piano. "No, I have not. And please do not think I am musical. I only learned to play because my mother considers it a necessary accomplishment for a girl."

"And so it is! Jamie, we must have some music lying about the place. It would be delightful if Catriona could give a little concert one evening!"

I could feel myself colouring. "Mrs McAllister, I must insist that you do not plan any such thing. I am an indifferent

189

pianist and do not play for company."

Jamie still had his head down, but he was looking at us from under his eyebrows, chuckling softly. "Well said, Cat! And you know, Grandmother, that old piano in the Great Hall hasn't been tuned for decades. I have no desire to hear *anyone* play it!"

Mrs McAllister's intention was to find me something to do that did not include Jamie. She could not have made it more obvious had she announced it. Undefeated, she leaned towards me. "Then what about reading?" she suggested. "Are you a novel reader, like me? Do you know Sir Walter Scott's books?"

"I do not, I am afraid. But I do like novels."

"Then *that* is how we shall spend this rainy afternoon! The library contains Scott's complete works. You may read aloud to me while I do my tapestry. *Catriona* – a most appropriate title, you will agree."

And so it came about that Jamie was allowed to do whatever he wished, and I was compelled to join his grandmother in the small drawing room and read Sir Walter Scott's novel about someone called Catriona while Mrs McAllister sewed a cushion cover, her spectacles on the end of her nose. Every so often she looked up and gave me an approving smile. At last, she had got her way. And I was powerless against her.

"That will be enough for now," she said after twenty pages or so. "Mark the place and we can go back to it tomorrow. Here, use this."

She handed me a length of tapestry wool. I slid it between the pages and closed the book with relief. But when I made to stand up, she gave me a stern look over her spectacles and motioned with her needle for me to sit down again. "Do not run away, Catriona. I wish to speak to you."

Dismayed, I waited while she knotted off her thread, placed her needle in the pin-cushion, removed her spectacles and put them in their case. "Now," she began, folding her hands upon the work in her lap, "in the short time you have been here, my grandson seems to have become rather fond of you."

I remained silent, clutching the book tightly between my palms to avoid betraying my agitation.

"You have made a profound impression on him," continued Mrs McAllister. Her green eyes looked at me steadily. She had something to say and was determined to say it. "Indeed, he is very impressionable. Perhaps more so than other young men. You see," she went on, before I could speak, "he has not been much in the world. He has no experience of young ladies."

I understood. She was telling me that he only liked me because I was the first girl he had ever met. This was undeniably rude, but to show myself offended would be to supply her with further ammunition. It would make me seem sure of myself, vain and flirtatious. "I suppose he does not," I said blankly.

"Furthermore, he adores his mother. He does not see her

often because the hospital distresses him. But he misses her dreadfully. Jamie is a loving boy, who has had nobody on whom to bestow his affection for some years. Is it any wonder that you have set his head spinning? "

Astonished, I gasped. "I have not done anything of the sort! Truly, I would not know how to set *anyone's* head spinning."

"But you are aware of his feelings for you?"

I felt my colour rise, but kept my voice steady. "Mrs McAllister, I can only suppose what Jamie feels. He appears to care for me, yes."

"But that does not mean you can set your cap at him!" All amiability was gone. Two pink spots had appeared on her cheekbones. "Hamish invited you here in order to set straight an old feud that is nothing to do with you. I would not have done so in his shoes, but he is the master of Drumwithie and may invite whomever he pleases. He did not expect you to…" As she searched for words, an idea came to her suddenly, setting her eyes ablaze. "This was cooked up between you and your mother, was it not? The instant she set eyes on Hamish, she planned for you to be mistress of Drumwithie. Do not deny it!" She was twisting her hands, creasing the tapestry, staring past my head, talking more to herself than to me. "And who would not exchange a modern house such as your father's, bought with money from trade, for an ancient estate, and a real, inherited fortune? I wanted the same for my own daughter and I achieved it! *She* is the present mistress of

192

Drumwithie, but the next one will *not* be you, Miss Catriona!"

I sat still, looking into her face. I hardly knew which of many emotions I felt most forcibly: rage, for the insult to my mother and myself; amazement at the tortuousness of Mrs McAllister's thoughts; and pity, for a woman to whom love meant nothing but an advantageous marriage. I had to clear my throat before I could speak. "And who *will* be the next mistress of Drumwithie?"

She had collected herself. Her face was resuming its usual pallor, and her voice was icy. "That is for destiny to decide. My grandson, as you are aware, is about to go up to university, where he will meet young ladies who are the daughters of more suitable families. You, meanwhile, will go back to Gilchester, where you belong."

She said the word with distaste, as if Gilchester were a place of such low social standing, she would have to be deranged to enter it. I smoothed my skirt while I considered how to reply, then I looked up at her. If my face showed defiance, I did not care. "Yes, I am aware that Jamie is on the brink of his new life. But I am younger even than he is and on the brink of *my* life too. I have no thought of making an alliance with anyone at present. And I must insist, Mrs McAllister, that you take back your accusation of my mother's ambition for me. I *absolutely* assure you that such a thing never entered her mind."

She had the grace to bow her head, though her expression did not change. "Very well, " she said.

"However," I continued before my courage failed me, "I refuse to apologize for the fact that Jamie has become fond of me. Love, I have heard it said, will run its course. And I intend to follow that course wherever it takes me."

Into her eyes came a different light. She stared at me, her mouth working. "You will regret this! You will find out, as your father did before you, that Drumwithie is an unlucky place for lovers!"

With that she got to her feet and, abandoning her work-basket, left the room.

I was too crushed to move. The fire burned low, but the room was warm now, and I did not replenish the coals. The afternoon dimmed almost to darkness, but I did not light the lamps.

Mrs McAllister's parting words about my father would not leave me. What could she have meant? She had never known my father. He had never visited Drumwithie as an adult. Doctor Hamish had clearly stated that the cousins had become estranged before "either of us had met our future wives". According to Jamie, Mrs McAllister knew about their falling-out, but as she had only begun to visit the castle after the doctor's courtship of her daughter had begun, she had never seen David Graham.

Staring into the fire, I remembered Mrs McAllister's face when Doctor Hamish had taken out Father's cigarette case. Troubled, agitated, full of dread. Why had she been so distressed, since she had never known the man to whom it had belonged?

I sat up, struck so forcefully by a thought that my ears buzzed. *If it were true she had never known my father, how did she recognize his cigarette case?*

My heart beat so hard the roar in my ears grew louder and louder. I tried to breathe deeply, but could not calm myself. My father's mother, Granny Graham, had given him that cigarette case when he was nineteen, and about to go up to Cambridge. But he and Doctor Hamish fell out soon afterwards and Father never went back to Drumwithie. So how did Mrs McAllister know the case had belonged to him? She had even referred to him as "David", which her cultivated manners would never allow her to do if she did not know him. Evidently, she *did* know him!

He must have come here, sometime after he went to Cambridge, perhaps during a university vacation. Contrary to what Doctor Hamish had told me, my father had met Mrs McAllister and, without doubt, her daughter Anne.

My eyes travelled irresistibly to the portrait above the mantelpiece. The beautiful, just-married Anne. Her husband's handsome, golden-haired cousin. Unchaperoned meetings. Ungovernable feelings. Unlawful love.

Numb, I stared at the portrait. *That* was why Mrs McAllister was so anxious to get me away from Jamie. "An old feud that is nothing to do with you," she had said. But the feud between our fathers *was* to do with me, and with Jamie. Handsome, golden-haired Jamie. Out of all the girls in the world, I was the one his grandmother could not allow him to fall in love with. It had nothing to do with my inferior wealth, my supposed desire to "set my cap" at the heir to Drumwithie. It was because there was a strong possibility that my father was Jamie's father too.

Jamie, I thought, my heart lurching. *Jamie, my love.* Like my father's before me, *my own unchaperoned, ungovernable, unlawful love.*

I sat by the fire for the rest of the afternoon. The gloom inside the castle and the lowering clouds outside made it as dark as it was possible for a place to be in daylight. The ruined tower was invisible, the trees a blur, the sky obliterated. It was banal to liken a wet day to sadness, but like many clichés, it contained a truth. Perhaps if the weather had been glorious, the weight upon my heart would not have felt so heavy.

Mrs McAllister did not return. At five o'clock, Jamie came in. "Why are you sitting in the dark?" he asked. But he did not stop to light the lamps. He squashed himself into the armchair beside me and put his arms around me. "Darling Cat, I have been lurking in the library all afternoon, thinking you were being subjected to some ghastly reading by my grandmother and impatient to talk to you – and here you are, all alone! However did you manage to get rid of her?"

I allowed my body to collapse against his. Whatever my dread about our possible blood relationship, Jamie remained Jamie. *My handsome winsome Johnny.* In his embrace I felt secure. "She got rid of herself," I told him. "Perhaps she was bored or had something else to do. Of course, the moment she left the room I put down that tedious book, and have been dozing by the fire."

He looked at me sideways. "You quarrelled. Do not deny it."

"Oh, Jamie, what nonsense you—"

"I can see it in your face, even by firelight," he insisted. He slid off the chair and sat at my feet. "You are not yourself. Your spirits are oppressed; there is something different about your eyes. You are not feeling ill, are you?"

What should I say? I could not speak of his grandmother's words, nor my suspicions about their significance. Jamie was unsettled enough; what if my fancy had run away with me, and the estrangement had been caused by something else entirely? "I do have a headache," I told him, glad of the excuse he had provided.

It was clear from his expression that I had not fooled him. He could see the uncertainty Mrs McAllister had planted in my mind. He was not as sure of my heart as he had been yesterday. "I suppose," he said, his eyes still searching my face, "a couple of hours spent reading aloud to my grandmother is enough to give anyone a headache!"

His tone was light, but I was not fooled either. "Jamie, my afternoon has not been pleasant, it is true, but apparently neither has yours, and *you* are perfectly well. My headache has nothing to do with that. It is just a headache."

To my relief, he did not pursue the point, but sat back on

his heels and patted his pockets for his cigarettes. "Actually," he said, "my afternoon was not as unpleasant as you think." He threw his match on the fire and regarded me through the cigarette smoke. "It was really rather extraordinary. Indeed, one might say wonderful." He drew on the cigarette, smiling enigmatically as he exhaled. "Though for once, the wonder has not been caused by the beautiful Cait Sìth."

Removing Mrs McAllister's crumpled tapestry from the other chair, he sat down and leaned towards me, his elbows on his knees. His hair had grown long enough by now to be brushed back and slicked down with water, and the firelight revealed his smooth, suntanned face without hindrance. I was touched, as always, by his eagerness and innocence.

"This afternoon," he began, "Father returned from the surgery earlier than usual. When he found me alone in the library, he asked to see some of my work. I was amazed. I said, 'Do you mean my *poetry*, Father?' He has never in his life called it my 'work' before. And what he said when he looked at it – while I sat with my back to him, rigid with fear, as you can imagine – was more amazing still. He said it was far better than he had imagined it would be. Then he started to talk about keeping an open mind, and not allowing his love of his own profession to stand in the way of his judgement. He said that the important thing is to get there in the end, even if the path is twisting. I must say, I've never heard him sound so reasonable."

Neither had I. But the words themselves I *had* heard before. At Chester House, when Doctor Hamish and Mother had discussed Jamie's several attempts to pass his examinations, Mother had made her usual comment about perseverance: "But he got there in the end, however twisting the path, and that is the important thing!" Unbeknown to Jamie and if only indirectly, the influence of the faerie cat *was* at work in his father's words.

"Jamie, that *is* wonderful. What did you say?"

"Well, I didn't have much hope, but I thought I'd chance it, so I asked him if he might consider my giving up the University altogether. I thought he'd give me his usual sour-faced lecture, but – this is scarcely believable, Cat, you may have to pinch me – he told me he had spoken on the telephone this afternoon to the Dean of the Medical School. Father and I have an appointment for tomorrow, to see this fellow and discuss retaining my place, but changing from medicine to a different subject!"

"Oh!" I flushed with surprise and pleasure. "This is the very outcome I myself have wished for! You see, your father is not such a pompous oaf after all!"

He looked at me happily, but ruefully. "And what subject do you think will suit a man with poetic ambitions? Shall I study history and become an eminent historian? Or found a publishing house? That would give me plenty of time for composition *and* ensure my poems are published! Failing that, I could write books on Scottish history and give public lectures – and open the ruined part of Drumwithie to the public on the first Sunday of every month!" He laughed gleefully. "What a lark! I would be known as 'That glaikit auld fuil, Buchanan o' Drumwithie'!" he added in his most exaggerated Scots.

I did not laugh. "Perhaps," I pointed out, "the choice of subject will be discussed at your meeting tomorrow."

"Aye," he said dreamily, leaning back in his chair. "And as long as it does not involve cutting up dead bodies, I do not care what it is." He looked at me from under lowered eyelids. "And now, you must tell me the real reason you are so out of spirits."

I smoothed my skirt. "So you and your father will be off to Edinburgh in the morning?"

"On the nine fifteen train. Father and Doctor Skerran over in Dunkeith share emergencies on Saturday afternoons and Sundays, and it is Doctor Skerran's turn tomorrow." He waved his cigarette theatrically. "Cat, this evasiveness is making me so very agitated! Is it the thought of going down to the cave? Has Grandmother been frightening you with her nonsense?"

"It is nothing to do with the cave."

I stood up and went to the window, glad to stretch my legs after sitting so long. Jamie followed and stood beside me. The rain had eased to a drizzle. The lawn was visible, and Anne's garden. Beyond that lay the valley, blue–green in the gathering dusk and absolutely still. How beautiful it was, and how mysterious.

"It is to do with Grandmother, though, is it not?"

He went to draw me towards him. His face was so full

of tenderness and love, my heart swelled. But the moment had come; I slid free of his embrace and leaned against the windowsill, weakened by the flood of emotions. "I am sorry," I said, but I do not... I cannot..."

"What is it, darling Cat?" He was so close to me, his breath dampened my cheek. "What ideas has she been putting into your head?"

"Nobody has put any ideas into my head!" I could not look at him. "But I have been thinking ... this dalliance may not be—"

"Dalliance!" He was offended. He stood back. "What, do you think I am a philanderer? My intention is not to *dally* with you, Cat! What an awful word – it reminds me of those sentimental songs about maids and soldiers kissing at the garden gate. What is the matter with you?"

I did not wish to witness his hurt. I closed my eyes, but could not stop tears welling behind my eyelids. I loved him; I knew I did, and he knew I did. But loving him might prove impossible. "Please understand—"

"Have no fear, I *do* understand!"

My eyes were stinging, but I dared not open them, in case the tears fell and alerted him to my misery. I stood with my back to him, fumbling in my sleeve for a handkerchief, sniffing and mumbling. "I am so sorry, Jamie. I am sorry I accused you of dalliance. That was an unforgiveable choice of word. I did not mean that I think you wish to take advantage of me or anything like that. I was only trying to explain that I am overwhelmed by my feelings, and yours."

Half blinded with tears, I turned and looked into his face. Fear was gathering in his eyes. He stepped closer. "I do not believe you," he said softly, no longer accusing. "Something has placed doubt in your mind. What the devil has happened?"

"Nothing!" I protested. "At least, all that has happened is that I have been sitting here thinking, and—"

"And you have decided that love is too precious to run at like a pole vaulter runs at the bar? You wish to cry 'Hold, hold!' like Lady Macbeth, in case our feelings carry us away? You think I am such a *puppy*, while you are the goddess of reason?"

I was too distressed to speak. Jamie crushed his cigarette angrily in an ashtray. "Do not try and pretend, Cat. You are hopeless at it. My grandmother obviously considers me a worthless bounder who wishes only to seduce you. I am not surprised at that. But what does surprise me is that you believe her!"

Although I had no reason to feel shame, his accusation humiliated me nonetheless. That he should think such a thing was intolerable. But I could not let him suspect that his grandmother had said not that *he* was unworthy of *me*, but that *I* was unworthy of *him*. Furthermore, her unguarded words about my father and my suspicions about Jamie's parentage must be kept from him at all costs.

My helplessness silenced me. I stood there, the warmth of

the glowing embers drying the tears on my cheeks, unable to defend either myself or Mrs McAllister. Jamie turned and grasped the edge of the mantelpiece with both hands, his head bowed beneath his mother's portrait. Perhaps he could no longer bear to look at me. But my heart expanded with love.

Together, Jamie and I had kept the secret of the ghost and felt our way towards its revelation: the tree, the cave, the rain, the slide. And all the while we had been feeling our way towards a true attachment to each other. But now, I had repulsed him. How disappointed he must be! At the exact moment when his father's change of mind had increased his happiness, my own apparent change of mind had begun to threaten it.

His breath came unevenly; he was angry and upset. I knew I could not leave him like this. I could no longer permit myself to feel the thrilling, abandoned happiness of yesterday, but my love, and desire for his love, endured regardless. "Jamie…" I ventured softly, "please hear me. Your grand-mother *did* speak to me about you, but she did not accuse you of philandering. She merely expressed her concern that we were rushing too quickly into an attachment, considering that we are both so young, and you are on the brink of your university career. She was quite sensible about it." I braced myself for the lie. "So sensible, I found myself almost agreeing with her."

He whipped round, astonished, but when he tried to

protest, I held up my hand. "Of course, she has no inkling of the depth of our feelings! But I must own the truth of her words, though it pained me to hear them. And so must you."

His eyes bore through me, suspicious still, but gleaming with that familiar, and beloved, excitement. After a long moment, he whispered, "You *do* love me, then?"

My throat constricted; I whispered too. "Of course I love you."

He looked at the ceiling, as if thanking some deity for his deliverance. Then he laughed. "Do you know what I wish, little Cat?" he said. "That we could run away together like people in stories, and live in an attic in Bloomsbury. I could be a poet and you could mend my shirts and cook my porridge, and my father and grandmother, and your mother, and the Dean of the Medical School and everyone else who thinks we are too young and irresponsible wouldn't be there, and it would be *heaven*."

"It would not." My voice had recovered, though my spirits had not. "And you know it. Listen to the goddess of reason."

He smiled at me. The anger of a moment ago had evaporated. "I will not kiss you, though God knows I want to! The puppy has been admonished and will behave himself."

THE CAVE

By the time I came down the next day, Jamie and the doctor had breakfasted and gone out, and Mrs McAllister did not appear. I had the castle to myself.

By the middle of the morning the rain had eased enough for a proper inspection of the landslide to be made. MacGregor came in, stamping his boots on the flagstones, and reported gloomily that it was worse than the slide of twenty years ago. "A whole section of the glenside is come away," he told me and Bridie. "I canna say how many trees are lost, but it's a braw few."

"May I go out and look?" I asked.

MacGregor looked doubtful. "Ye ken 'tis dangerous down there, miss, do ye not?"

"I will not venture down the glen. Is it still raining?"

"Aye, ye'll need a mackintosh."

Bridie went to the boot room and returned with an oilskin. "Here ye are, miss. This is Mr Jamie's, so it'll be too big, but it'll keep ye nice and dry." She addressed MacGregor as she helped me into the oilskin. "Go with Miss Graham and the both of ye's be careful, now."

Five minutes later, I left the house for the first time in three days. MacGregor and I made our way under dripping branches to Anne's garden and looked over the wall.

Shocked, I stared into the depths. Mud, stones, bracken, gorse, grass, heather and the bright green moss that grew between the boulders lay tangled together on the hillside, like rubbish thrown out by a giant. And the trees, so majestic when they stood, had been tossed aside like driftwood. Pines, rowans and birches had met their ends, their roots, still embedded in lumps of earth, held aloft. Their leaves and branches were impossible to separate; all I could see was a soaking wet mass of blackish-green vegetation.

Jamie and I would never be able to get down to the cave. Even if we had MacGregor's help with ropes and ladders, Doctor Hamish would never give his permission. And even if he could be persuaded, Mrs McAllister, who disapproved of the caves, would do everything she could to stop us.

I swayed and had to hold on to the wall.

"Are ye faint, miss?" Macgregor took a step towards me, ready to catch me if I fell.

"No, thank you. It is only the sight of all this destruction."

He was satisfied and stood back. But it was not the state of the glenside that had affected me. It was my sudden conviction that Mrs McAllister did not want anyone going into the cave because there was something there she did not want discovered. Something, perhaps, to do with my father's final visit to Drumwithie, and the long-kept secret he had left behind.

"Where are you, Cat!" Jamie's boots crashed across the hall and he threw open the library door. I was sitting on the window seat, lost in my thoughts, my book abandoned on my lap.

"I was so nervous!" he cried. "And this fellow, this Dean or whatever he was, was an awful fop. I never trust a man who wears a monocle. But apparently he has the ear of the committee."

"So the meeting was a success?"

"Well, he is writing to Father. The Dean of Humanities has to approve my application to study history. It is all pieces of paper, you know, being passed around between old men in old buildings." He was standing in front of the fire, warming his hands. "And how have you spent your morning?"

"Making a discovery, actually."

He sat down, interested.

"I went out with MacGregor and looked at the slide."

"Indeed?" His eyes widened.

"A great deal of ground has fallen away, taking many trees with it. They are jumbled up on top of each other, farther down the slope."

"What about the oak tree? Could you see it?"

"Not from the top, no. And, Jamie, it is quite impossible to get down the side of the glen."

"Nonsense!" He pushed back his hair in irritation. "You have been listening to MacGregor, haven't you? He never wants to do any more work than he has to."

"MacGregor said nothing about it. It was clear to me that we cannot attempt it."

"I will find that cave if I have to die in the process!"

"Jamie, now *you* are talking nonsense." I swung my legs off the window seat and leaned towards him. "Listen to me. We cannot go. It is too dangerous."

He looked at me sorrowfully. "I am not afraid of the danger and neither are you. That look is on your face again, the one you had yesterday, when you were trying to tell me something you did not believe."

I sat back, feeling foolish. "I believe such an expedition will be foolhardy."

"So you would abandon the ghost's request?"

"Do not accuse me of that!"

"Then tell me the truth!"

I hesitated, hovering over my next sentence, wishing to persuade, not disappoint him. "We have very little information to go on. Even if we manage to get into the cave, we do not know what to look for. And even if we find something, we may not understand its significance. The ghost seemed to indicate the pine tree that marks the cave, but for all we know we have mistaken her meaning. We may do more harm than good."

His eyes narrowed. "We have not mistaken her meaning. You told me she confirmed that we were correct. You agreed you must come with me to the cave. But now you are saying neither of us should go! Where has your curiosity gone?"

Confounded by the logic of this argument, I decided to confess some of the truth. "I am still curious, of course. But I am anxious about what might be down there. What if we discover something that is better left undiscovered?"

He gazed at me, frowning slightly, his eyes busy. He could not fathom what I might mean. I suppressed feelings of disloyalty and the desire to blurt out my true fear, that the cave might contain secrets too hurtful for Jamie to bear. I tried one more feeble protest. "And anyway, we shall never get permission."

"We do not need permission. We shall go after dark."

"What?"

He smiled thinly at my loss of composure. "You, of all creatures, should be at home in the darkness." He held out his hand and I instinctively took it. "Without you, Cat, none of this would have happened. The ghost needs you to see it through to its end. I do not understand your fears, but you will not let her down, will you?"

I had never been outside in the middle of the night before.

At one o'clock in the morning, I slid out of bed. I put on Jamie's old clothes, covered my hair with a scarf and crept down the spiral stairs to the silent darkness of the landing. No moon shone; the clouds were too thick. But there was a sliver of light under Jamie's sitting-room door. I did not need to knock. He was waiting for me.

He sat in a pool of lamplight at the table, wearing his jacket and cap, surrounded as usual by books and writing paper. When I entered he smiled with delight. Perhaps, right up until the last minute, he had not been sure I would come.

We did not speak as we made our way down the stairs and into the boot room. Once the door was closed behind us, Jamie took something from his pocket. In an instant, a beam of light flashed around the small room, brightest at its centre, but casting a halo around Jamie pointed it. I gasped. "What is *that*?"

"It is called a flashlight." He turned it on his face so I could see that he was grinning. The beam gave him an eerie look, throwing the planes and hollows of his face into relief, as if painted for the stage. "An American invention. I stole it from Father's desk when he was at work. Isn't it a wonderful thing? No gas, no oil, no matches, not even any wires. You can take it anywhere and it will light your way."

So he planned to visit the cave with the aid of a disembodied light, a torch with no flame. "What makes it work?" I asked, not quite believing him.

"Electricity, stored in these things called batteries. When they stop working, you put new ones in." He reached into his other pocket and took out two cylindrical metal objects with *The Ever Ready Electrical Company* printed on the sides. He looked at me triumphantly. "And I stole the spare batteries too!"

I was impressed. "Very well," I whispered as we tied our bootlaces by the light of the machine, "but I wish you had a flashlight for *me*."

"One is enough," said Jamie decisively, "because I will lead the way. Now, are you ready? The outside door is locked, but the window is merely latched. The sill is not too high for you, is it? Shall I lift you?"

The window was an ordinary square casement, about two feet wide. I could climb through such a space, if Jamie could. "The sill is not too high," I told him. But as he reached for the window latch, I spoke again. "Jamie, what if the land slides again? What if we are injured, or killed?"

"Then I will die by the side of the woman I love!" he declared melodramatically. "But it will not happen," he added, grinning. "I do not intend to die until I have astonished the world with my literary achievements. And like the best poets, I will meet my end by contracting tuberculosis or syphilis." He paused. "Alternatively, I will do it by means of a flying accident."

I clambered after him out of the window and dropped to my knees on the grass outside. It was so sodden with rainwater, the old trousers I wore were immediately wetted through. "Ugh!" I cried.

"*Sshh!*" He turned the flashlight off and in the darkness,

we listened. Silence. Not even an owl's cry. Nothing but the scent of the pine trees and the blackness of the chasm below Drumwithie's rock.

Satisfied that no one had heard us, Jamie switched on the flashlight again, holding it close by his side, his fingers partly obscuring the beam. I held his other hand while we crossed the bridge and the patch of gorse to the lip of the valley. When we were out of sight of the house, he shone the full beam before us, swinging it from side to side, illuminating the swathe of damage the rainstorm had done. It was a scar on the glen side, but happily enough, the slide had left the terrain more accessible. We no longer had to fight under-growth or the low branches of trees, because much of what had been there before had disappeared down the hill.

We made surprisingly good progress. The ledge on which the tall pine tree stood had survived the slide, and the tree was still there, though the ground was no longer a carpet of pine needles. Debris lay all around it, stacked several feet up its trunk on the sloping side. In the artificial yellow–white of the flashlight beam, the stones and broken branches looked unreal, painted in the wrong colours.

Jamie stepped towards the edge, testing the ground before putting his weight on it. The mud was slippery, but under it was an outcrop of solid rock. "It is quite safe," he said.

I looked over the edge. I could not see the cave entrance, but below us there was a clear path, carved horizontally along the valley side.

"You see?" said Jamie in excitement. "That is the path the tree fell across. Come on!"

Half stepping, half sliding, I followed him down the scree of mud and stones beneath the rock. Once our feet were on the path, the ground was level. Jamie pointed the flashlight. "Look!"

Where the great oak had lain for so many years there was a muddy, stony gap in the path. Beside it was a huge boulder, bigger than those that guarded the entrance to the other caves. And above that boulder was another, which stooped over the lower one like a protective parent. Between them, blacker than any of the surrounding blackness, was what could only be the entrance to the cave. Jamie gripped my hand, held the flashlight aloft, and we climbed in.

I do not know what I expected. Damp, slimy walls, years of dirt on the floor, bats and other nocturnal creatures, stalagmites and stalactites? I saw none of these. Before us lay what could only be described as a room. Protected from the elements by the two boulders, the cave had remained dry, as if it were a man-made outhouse instead of a natural feature. Jamie had told me that the caves under the castle had been used for storage for centuries, because they were so cold. This cave looked as though it could perform the function today.

The walls were of uneven rock, like the walls of the other caves, but the floor was level and the ceiling high enough for us to walk upright. We stood and looked around.

"There is nothing here," I observed breathlessly. "Shall we go back now?"

Jamie ignored my suggestion. He shone the flashlight on the back wall. Deep in the cave, we saw a hole in the rock, just above the floor. Jamie knelt down and shone the flashlight. "It must lead to another cave."

Kneeling beside him, I peered in. The hole was small, but not too small for a slim person to enter.

"You are smaller than I am," he said. "You had better go in."

"Why? There is nothing there."

"How do you know that?" he asked in exasperation. "Stop being so nonsensical!"

He gave me the flashlight. The only way I could enter the hole was to lie on my stomach and crawl in, using my elbows to propel myself. Through my sleeves and trousers, my flesh was grazed by the rough surface of the rock. Inside, the ceiling was high enough for me to get to my feet, though I had to bend double. I took a few steps, then a few more, and suddenly the beam of the flashlight revealed a wall. I had come to the end of the passageway. When I saw what had been placed at the foot of the wall, my heart turned over. A ladies' travelling box sat in polished-walnut splendour on the ancient floor.

This was what I had dreaded. A hiding place full of secrets. A box containing … what? Letters between those long-ago lovers, my father and Jamie's mother? Evidence that Doctor

Hamish was not telling the truth when he said that they had never met? Proof, once and for all, that Anne had kept a secret from her husband for twenty-one years, a secret so burdensome it had ruined her peace, and would now ruin Jamie's?

My breath came jerkily. I had been handed the perfect solution. All I had to do was crawl back out of the second cave, feigning disappointment, and tell Jamie that there was nothing there. I would have to abandon the ghost and find an excuse to go back to Gilchester as soon as possible. At the end of the summer Jamie would go to university, and meet the sort of girls his grandmother wished him to meet. Gradually our letters would become infrequent, then cease. My heart would break, but Anne Hamilton's secret would be safe for ever.

I turned to go out the way I had come, but as the flashlight beam wheeled round, I yelped in surprise. A face was emerging from the darkness of the narrow passageway. Only the face, though, and one arm; the rest of Jamie's body was still in the hole. "I can't get my other shoulder through!" he lamented.

"What are you doing?" I kept the flashlight on his face, hoping it would blind him to the box.

"I called to you but you didn't hear, and I thought something might have happened to you. Are you all right? Get that light out of my eyes, will you, so I can see!"

When I did not, he lost patience. He could just reach me.

His arm landed on my wrist like a battering-ram and knocked the flashlight from my hand. The suddenness of his action reminded me of the moment when he had hurled the lantern at the wall of the cave below the well. I shrieked, terrified that the flashlight would smash, and we would be left in the worst darkness I had ever known. But Providence was with me. The light did not go out. Jamie grasped it and shone it round the cave. "What's that? A box? Cat, there's a box in here!"

"You hurt me," I told him, nursing my wrist. I felt cold, stupid, defeated. All I could hope was that the box was empty or full of ladies' travelling things. "There was no need to do that. You are impossible!"

"Sorry," he said, not sounding in the least sorry. His eyes followed the flashlight beam around the cave. "Did you find anything else?"

"No."

"Then let's get this box out. You push and I'll pull."

The box was quite light, though cumbersome in the small space. We manhandled it through the hole and I clambered out. Jamie placed the box on the smooth floor, propping the flashlight beside it. His trembling fingers travelled fruitlessly over the lid and sides. He could not open it.

"It must be locked, damn it," he muttered in frustration. "But there's no keyhole. How the devil do we open it?"

"I know how." There was little point in pretending. If we did not open the box by the proper means, Jamie would take an axe to it. "My grandmother had such a box."

I held it by the two front corners and squeezed with my thumb and forefinger. The mechanism inside slid along its groove and I lifted the lid. "It was designed to stop servants discovering secrets," I told Jamie, propping the lid open with its little brass bracket. "Granny liked it because she didn't have to remember where the key was."

The inside of the lid was mirrored, and the box had four compartments, where bottles and brushes for a lady's toilette had originally been stored. These had gone, and in their place were several pieces of folded paper, stacked in piles.

I eyed them in dread. Was I about to see my father's familiar handwriting? My nerve failed me. I could not bear for Jamie and, worse still, Doctor Hamish, to discover what I suspected. "Please, Jamie," I pleaded, "these things are clearly someone's secrets. Do you not think we should leave them alone?"

"Of course not." He scooped one pile out of its compartment. It was a collection of yellowing newspaper cuttings, tattered with age. "Now we have come this far, how can we leave them unread?" He turned the bundle over and over in his hand. "These cuttings are obviously important enough for someone to hide them down here. They must be about something scandalous, or at least *interesting*, Cat. How can you stand not to know what it is?"

Relief rushed over me. He was right; the contents of the box were more likely to commemorate some public event than the private one I had feared.

"Good God, listen!" He had opened the first. "This is from *The Scotsman*, dated 1st February, 1888. The headline is *Advertisement by Family of Missing Girl*, and then it goes on to say, *Mrs Jean McAllister of Drumwithie, Lothian, widow of the late Reverend Herbert McAllister of Stirling, has placed an advertisement in this newspaper, and in several other newspapers throughout the British Isles. Information is sought as to the whereabouts of her daughter, Miss Lucy McAllister, 16, who was last seen on 8th December last year. Her disappearance is a source of great distress to Mrs McAllister and her elder daughter, Miss Anne McAllister, who wait daily for news. Please see the advertisement on page 12 for further information.*

Jamie was staring at me, his eyes wider and wilder than I had ever seen them. "*Lucy McAllister?* This cannot be right. There is no Lucy. My mother has no sister." He consulted the cutting again. "Sixteen! Younger than you! If Mother had a sister, why does Father not know of her?" His eyes clouded in bewilderment. "And if he *does*, why has he never..." He looked again at the scrap of paper in his hand. "They have kept her existence secret from me, haven't they? For God's sake, Cat, why would they do that?"

Revulsion suddenly took hold of me. I did not wish to be in this pseudo-room hewn from rock, leafing through old secrets in the eerie, yellow light. I had no desire to know if Jamie had an aunt or what had happened to her. I longed only for my bed. "It must be very late by now," I said urgently. "And I am very cold. Shall we take these things away with us, and read them in daylight, in the house?"

He was reluctant, but he began to take the bundles of papers from the box, and put them in the inside pockets of his jacket. "I suppose we had better leave the box here, then." He held out a bundle to me. "Put some in the pockets of those trousers."

I took the papers from his grasp, but missed my grip and they tumbled to the floor. Lying on the top of the scattered pile was a cutting of the advertisement Mrs McAllister had put in *The Scotsman*. I took hold of it and gazed in astonishment.

Above Lucy McAllister's name were the words, *Have you seen this girl?* And from the photograph below it gazed a very familiar face. Pale, with almond-shaped eyes and a tangle of dark hair, arranged loosely over the shoulders of an old-fashioned, apron-fronted silk dress.

THE SPELL IS WOUND

Lucy McAllister had disappeared on the night of 8th December, 1887.

It had been a snowy night, and windy, with deep drifts forming. According to the newspaper reports Jamie and I pored over the next morning in his sitting room, her mother and sister saw her that day. They breakfasted together as usual at their cottage in Drumwithie, where they had moved from Stirling after the death of the Reverend McAllister. The elder Miss McAllister, recently engaged to be married to Dr Hamish Buchanan of Drumwithie Castle, had spent the morning sewing her trousseau, while her mother, who was recovering from a bad cold, rested and read the newspaper by the fire. Lucy, an enthusiastic artist, went to her room to work on a drawing. But when she did not appear for luncheon, it was discovered that her cloak and boots had gone, and it was assumed that despite the inclement weather, she had gone out.

She did not come back that day, or the day after. A search party was dispatched, but nothing was found. Surprisingly, she had taken no luggage with her. All her indoor clothes except her best dress, a pink silk in which she had been photographed only a week before her disappearance, were in her wardrobe. No one could understand why a young girl, happily settled in a loving family, might put on her best dress and go out in the snow, to disappear without trace.

"Until her ghost appears in the tower room of Drumwithie Castle, almost twenty-three years later," said Jamie, returning a cutting to the table and leaning back in his chair. "Damn it, Cat, I am absolutely mystified."

I was browsing through the other papers. Not all were cuttings; there were photographs and a few letters. The first photograph I showed Jamie made us look at each other sorrowfully. It was an official wedding photograph, mounted on stiff card. Below it were the printed words, "The marriage of Dr Hamish Buchanan of Drumwithie Castle, only son of the late Mr and Mrs Charles Buchanan, and Miss Anne McAllister, elder daughter of the late Reverend Herbert McAllister and Mrs Jean McAllister of Drumwithie. 20th February, 1888."

The young Hamish and the even younger Anne stared stiffly into the camera, her long train spread around her, his top hat tilted at the angle favoured by fashionable young Victorians. Beside them stood a slimmer Mrs McAllister, dressed like a duchess in silk damask. Behind were ranged a collection of unrecognizable people, possibly uncles or cousins. My father was not present, though this was before he and Doctor Hamish fell out. Perhaps because of Lucy's absence, there was no bridesmaid.

"Good God," breathed Jamie bleakly, "I have never seen this before."

I studied the print. "It is those words, Jamie. 'Elder daughter.' If they wished to keep Lucy secret from you, they could not show you this photograph."

He examined it too. "They could have separated it from the mount, I suppose," he said discontentedly. "But no, I am at fault. I should have wondered why there were no pictures of my parents' wedding in the house. But I did not. I never wondered and I never asked."

I held out another photograph. "Look, here is the picture that was used for the newspaper advertisement. Do you think Lucy looks like your mother?"

"They have the same nose. They probably look like each other in profile."

Of course! I knew where I had seen the ragged ghost's profile before – in the portrait of Anne that hung in the small drawing room. "Tell me who you are!" I had begged the ghost, wondering if she was some forgotten acquaintance. "They do," I confirmed.

We looked at the photograph of Jamie's unknown aunt. Jamie seemed calmer. He sighed a little, turning the picture round and round in his fingers. "Perhaps she ran away because

someone had ruined her and she could not face the shame."
He looked at me with a measured, almost amused expression
in his face. "If I had the choice of telling my grandmother or
running away, I know which I would do!"

This sounded plausible, though I had a question. "Why run
away wearing your best dress and carrying no luggage?" Even
Jane Eyre, distressed beyond endurance by her experience with
the bigamist Edward Rochester, had not done that. But before
Jamie could speak, the thought of Jane Eyre's predicament
thrust an answer into my mind. "Oh!" I laid my hand on
his arm. "Do you think she might have been running away *to
meet* someone, to get married? And he jilted her? Oh, poor
Lucy!"

He smiled and covered my hand with his. "My dearest, I
fear you are turning the poor girl's story into one of your
penny dreadfuls."

Offended, I withdrew my hand. "For the last time, I do *not*
read penny dreadfuls! I am speculating about what might
have happened, exactly as you are yourself."

"Very well. I am contrite."

He did not look or sound contrite. I turned back to the
bundles of papers. "Shall we look at these letters?" I picked
up the nearest yellowing envelope, postmarked August 1887.
The address read, *Miss A. E. McAllister, Auchinleck Cottage,
Drumwithie, Lothian.* I drew out the letter and unfolded it. It
was from Lucy McAllister to her elder sister, written a few
months before she went missing.

Jamie moved close to my shoulder. I held the page where he could see it, and we read the letter through. The words were so simple, and the sentiments so heartfelt, it was as if the sixteen-year-old writer were standing there beside us.

London, Saturday, 5 o'clock

Dear Anne,

We are leaving shortly for the station. Indeed, unless I catch the quarter past five post, we may reach Drumwithie before this letter does. The enterprise has been a failure. I am depressed beyond description, but Mother insists it is merely a setback and I will get to Paris yet. Look for us tomorrow evening after eight o'clock, and have the kettle on for tea.

With affection,

Lucy

P.S. If any letters have come for me while we were away, I hope you have put them under my mattress, as we arranged. If not, I implore you, do it now!

Jamie and I looked at each other. "So-o-o," he said, frowning, "my mother knew her sister was corresponding with someone in secret. It looks as if your theory is not so far-fetched after all."

I was only half-listening. I had put Lucy's letter down and was already searching through the papers for the remaining letters. "Look!" I held one up in triumph. "From *Paris!*" I scrutinized the envelope. "Actually, the letter is *to* her, not *from* her." I drew the letter out. "It is from a man, someone called…" – I turned to the last page – "Matthieu. Do you read French well enough to understand it? I am sure I do not."

"I am very rusty," admitted Jamie. "Maybe there are other letters, in English."

We began to sort through and open envelopes. There were three letters from Matthieu, all of them in French. Jamie fetched his French dictionary. Luckily the other two letters were much shorter than the first one we had opened. By the time the clock struck twelve, we had deciphered enough to know that Matthieu was a young man living in his parents' house in Paris, stifled by bourgeois society and longing for his only love, Lucy. It was not clear how they had met. A great many artists were mentioned in his long letter; he had been to an exhibition which had fired him with enthusiasm, and looked forward to the time when he could set up his own studio and pursue the life of an artist himself. His parents wanted him to study engineering, the thought of which made him distraught.

"How history repeats itself!" said Jamie wistfully as he folded up the letters and returned them to their envelopes. "I wonder what happened to poor Matthieu. He must be forty or more by now."

My father's life had lasted only forty years. "I hope he is alive," I reflected. "Anyway, it looks as if Lucy might have wanted to study Art in Paris and be with her Matthieu. What could the failed enterprise in London be, I wonder?"

Jamie sat down in his fireside chair and rested his cheek on his hand. He looked tired, but his eyes also showed bewilderment. The contents of the box had disturbed him profoundly.

"I cannot think," he admitted. "I am weary of this, Cat. My brain is going round and round."

I picked up the next bundle, which was another collection of newspaper cuttings. "I am weary too. But I am determined to find out more."

My determination was born of two things: relief that the box did not contain anything about my father, and an overwhelming feeling of affinity with Lucy. The very first time her spirit had visited me, I had felt that although she had no voice she was speaking to me, and me alone. She was my age, she was dark-haired like me. She almost *was* me, but a version of me that inhabited a netherworld I could not cross into until my time came. I needed, for the sake of my own peace, to find out why she had appeared – dirty, ragged, beseeching me to help her – in my bedroom, *and only to me.*

I knelt down on the hearthrug. "How did she die, I wonder? And more to the point, if she had run away, perhaps as far as Paris, how did she come to die in the tower room here at Drumwithie?"

Somewhere downstairs, a door slammed. With a glance at

the clock Jamie gave me back the letter. "Grandmother is coming for luncheon today." His tone was resigned. "That is probably Bridie bustling about, though she does not usually slam doors. I hope she and MacGregor have not had a disagreement. He can be quite—"

His words were obliterated by heavy footsteps in the corridor and the door burst open. Doctor Hamish stood there, still in his riding coat, his face reddened with exertion. "Jamie, thank God you're here!"

In three strides, taking no notice of me, and seeming not to see the letters and photographs spread on the table, the doctor crossed the room to where his son sat. He looked troubled, his eyes almost wild. "We must go to the hospital immediately. Make haste."

Jamie had sprung up. "Has something happened to Mother?"

"I am afraid so. Doctor Galway telephoned me at the surgery. Grandmother is waiting downstairs. Come along."

"May Cat come too?" asked Jamie, throwing me a panicked look as he seized his cap and scarf.

I had risen from the rug and stood before the fireplace. Doctor Hamish's gaze found me. He looked bewildered, as if he were surprised to see me there. Then he collected himself. "It is family business," he said briskly.

"But Cat *is* family!" protested Jamie.

"Nevertheless, she may not come."

"I do not wish to," I put in, hoping to calm both of them.

"I have some tidying to do here, and then I will wait down-stairs for news."

"Very well, my dear," said the doctor distractedly.

"Shall Bridie wait luncheon?" I asked stupidly as they hurried from the room.

"No," said Doctor Hamish without pausing. "Tell her we shall be out all day."

When they had gone I looked again at Lucy's photograph. I studied her eyes, wondering what emotions were playing behind them on that day when she had posed in the photo-grapher's studio, her best dress arranged around her ankles and her hat tipped forward becomingly. Did she dream of her Frenchman? What had happened to him, and to her? And in what circumstances, young as she was, had she died?

I put the photograph with the other papers. Then, as good as my word, I tidied them away at the back of a drawer in Jamie's desk and went to tell Bridie about luncheon.

They did not return that day. At half past one Bridie, doing her best to remain cheerful, served me a solitary meal of soup and cold chicken. I could not finish it. Towards evening, a boy on a bicycle brought a telegram. Bridie passed it to me silently as she shut the front door. MacGregor had come in. They stood expectantly as I opened it.

I had never received a telegram before. I felt as if I were an actress, alone on stage at some crucial place in the play. I could not look at my audience. I read the message; it contained the bad news I had feared. "I am very sorry, but Mrs Buchanan has passed away," I told them. "The doctor says they are putting up at the Caledonian Hotel tonight. They will be home tomorrow on the eleven o'clock train."

MacGregor seemed dissatisfied. He stepped forward and for a moment I thought he was going to pluck the telegram from my hand to read for himself. He did not, but he looked at me accusingly. "No mention of how Mrs Buchanan passed away, then? Or when?"

"No, I'm afraid not. It just says, *Bereaved. Caledonian Hotel tonight. Home tomorrow 11 a.m. train.*" Telegrams, as my mother often observed, were cryptic enough to be almost ill-mannered. But Drumwithie had no telephone. When Doctor Hamish was needed out of surgery hours, the villagers summoned him the old-fashioned way, by riding up to the castle on a horse or a bicycle, or driving in a trap. "No doubt," I suggested, my voice shaking a little, "the doctor wishes to tell us in person what happened."

Bridie began to cry. She did not, as maids are popularly supposed to do, put her apron to her eyes and run out of the room. She stood there in the dimly lit hallway, sniffing and snorting, her pinky-gold face crumpling as we watched. "She'll be at peace!" she sobbed. "She'll be at peace at last!"

Her distress was as uninhibited as that of a child, and just as if she had been a child, I felt no awkwardness when I put my arms around her shoulders. The social chasm between the middle-aged woman and the young girl, the servant and the lady, vanished. Shorter in stature than I was, she leaned her head into my neck, wetting it with her tears.

I understood Bridie's spectacular grief. She had worked for Hamish and Anne Buchanan for a long time, probably since they married. She loved her mistress as she loved Jamie. She had watched the young Anne become ill; she had been present on, as Jamie had described it, the worst Wednesday of their lives. She had taken over the care of Jamie when his mother had eventually gone to the hospital. Had she visited her mistress there, I wondered, whether alone or with the boy?

I wished I could open the door to the past and witness what Bridie, and no doubt MacGregor too, had endured. I wished I could be of help to them. But they were unaware that Jamie had told me about his mother's illness at all.

"Yes, it is all over now," I assured Bridie. "She is not suffering any more."

Bridie made no reply. Her sobbing had lessened, but I could still feel her shoulders trembling. When she drew back from my embrace, I proffered my handkerchief. She took it and blew her nose.

"You must go to your room now and rest," I told her.

"Aye, miss."

Bridie was leaning against the door jamb, the handkerchief at her eyes. MacGregor stood silently by, as if awaiting instructions. Suddenly I understood that in the absence of everyone else, I had been thrust into the role of mistress of

Drumwithie for this one strange evening. Daunted, but unwilling to let the gillie see it, I nodded briskly. "We must all pass this evening as best we can, MacGregor, and see what the morning brings," I told him. "Lock up as usual, and please would you meet the eleven o'clock train tomorrow."

He gave a small bow. His eyes, I noticed, were misted. Perhaps he would go into the boot room and weep for Anne Buchanan too.

With that we parted. I took the telegram to the tower room and reread it. The stark words gave no clue as to the nature of Jamie's mother's death. All we knew was that Anne, while still a young woman like her sister before her, had quitted the world and left those who loved her bereaved.

I sat down at the table, my body limp with a surge of grief. Not only for Anne herself, but for Doctor Hamish, for Jamie and, above all, for Mrs McAllister. She had lost her younger daughter when Lucy had barely reached adulthood. And now, in this latest unhappy turn of fate, her elder daughter had gone too, after years of harrowing illness and an attempted suicide.

I frowned, thinking hard. It was well documented that those who attempted suicide once often attempted it again. That was why mentally unstable patients were placed in special hospitals, such as the one Anne was in, where they could be kept safe. But supposing – oh, dear God! – supposing the hospital had failed to protect Anne from self-destruction?

Very agitated, I stood up and opened the tower-room door.

It was not yet dark outside, though the clouds were low. The castle suddenly seemed a prison, full of oppressed souls. I hurried down the stairs and across the flagstones, out of the main door and over the bridge. The twilit air was humid; the threat of rain had not yet passed. The dark green of the trees was an irregular scar on the glenside, mingling in my mind the beauty of Drumwithie with the disquieting memory of the pine tree which had shown the way to the cave, and the identity of my ghostly visitor.

I began to run. My whole being tingled with the desire to move, as quickly as possible, in any direction. No thoughts formed. It was as if my bones, muscles, blood and brain wished to exhaust themselves without my permission; I wanted to run and run until I collapsed.

But I had not the strength. Before I had gone more than a few yards beyond the garden, I fell to my knees among the broom bushes and covered my face with my hands, filled with despair. Shock rushed in upon me like a hurricane. I could not stop myself trembling, but I could not cry. I knelt there, rocking on my heels, powerless against dark thoughts.

Jamie, beloved of so many people, standing bereft of his adored mother at the very doorstep of his life.

Jamie, my love, yet perhaps never my love.

I took my hands away from my eyes. The gloaming fell fast, but the landscape around me had not yet darkened completely. In the castle windows, a few lights burned, in Bridie's room, and the hall, and the upstairs landing. The kitchen and boot-room windows were dark; MacGregor must have gone to the tavern in Drumwithie. I did not blame him. I wished for oblivion myself. Slowly, I got to my feet.

And suddenly, I saw it. Not a vision, or a memory, or something imagined, but a revelation. It tumbled down on me, as unexpected as a cloudburst, with such force that I gasped.

When a human child was taken, every seven years a payment had to be made to the devil. The *teind*, Mrs McAllister had called it.

When Jamie was seven years old, his mother had suffered a nervous breakdown.

When he was fourteen, she had tried to kill herself.

Now, when he was twenty-one, she had died.

What had happened in the missing seventh year, the year Jamie, a fair-haired faerie child, perhaps the secret son of a fair-haired lover, was born?

Who had suffered for the devil's promise?

I scrambled up the hillside, the gorse bushes scratching my neck and arms. Letting myself in by the back door, I hurried through the darkness to the kitchen yard. In the corner, the stone staircase that led to the servants' quarters bit deep into the tower, winding through the thick stone so that servants could get to the guest bedroom unobtrusively. I sometimes used this back staircase when I had no wish to meet anyone between the garden and my room – Mrs McAllister in particular. Tonight, I had a different reason to use it.

The staircase was dark. This older wing behind the kitchen was still lit only by candles and oil lamps. No one had ever installed lights on the walls; Bridie and MacGregor carried candles to their quarters, hers on this uncarpeted landing, his above the stable yard, as servants had done for hundreds of years. I made my way cautiously, feeling for the rope banister. The stairs were not only dark, they were narrow, and colder even than the rest of the house. I had not stopped to put my shawl around my shoulders; goosebumps raised the hairs on my arms, and I had to clamp my teeth together to stop my jaw trembling. I was cold, but I was also consumed by some other sensation. Not fear exactly, but fearful expectation.

A faint light came from under Bridie's door. I hesitated a moment, then knocked. The door opened a little, and half of Bridie's face appeared. Her one visible eye looked swollen with crying. "Aye, miss?"

"I am sorry to disturb you, Bridie, but may I have a word with you?"

She opened the door wider; I saw she was carrying a candle in a brass holder. I entered the room and she shut the door silently after me. Then she gestured to a wicker chair beside the narrow bed. I seated myself, and she climbed onto the bed, sitting with her back against the wall, her knees drawn up under her skirt. She had taken off her apron and loosened her hair. The candlelight threw her face into relief; I saw shadows in it I had not noticed before. She looked older than her forty or so years, and her eyes were blank with uncomprehending misery. My presence seemed to summon further grief. She began to cry quietly into an already sodden handkerchief.

"Bridie," I began awkwardly, "I must ask you something."

She wiped her eyes ineffectually and raised her head, but said nothing.

"It is about Mr Jamie," I told her.

"Aye," she whispered. She crumpled the handkerchief into a damp ball, so tightly that her fingers showed white, and brought it to her lips. "I ken what ye're wanting to say, miss."

How could she know? My heart murmured as I spoke. "You have known him all his life, have you not?"

She nodded.

"Then perhaps you can help me understand why Mr Jamie sometimes does things that are … impulsive, and says strange things. He seems at odds with the world."

She gazed at me steadily. Her eyes were bright with tears. "Ye canna leave him, miss!" She drew a shaky breath and released it with a shudder. "It's yersel', and only yersel', that'll be the one for him. Now his mother's gone, he must have yersel', or nobody!"

I stared at her, my brain numb with astonishment.

"Ye'll no tell what I said, will ye, if ye please, miss?" she pleaded.

"I will not tell." I leant towards her. "But I do not understand what you mean. Why do you say that now his mother has died Mr Jamie needs me?"

She dropped her gaze. I could not tell if she was embarrassed, or ashamed, or fearful that I would scold her. I summoned my courage. "Bridie, are you aware that he and I have formed an attachment?"

"Aye, miss. It's been as plain as plain from the day ye arrived."

"But ... whether I wish to or not, I will have to leave Drumwithie when Mr Jamie goes off to Edinburgh in the autumn."

Her face took on an anguished look, as if I had suggested something so intolerable it caused her physical pain. "But there's nobody else can *free* him, miss! Ye *mustna'* leave him, *ever!*"

I was aware that I felt chillier than I had before. Bridie's fire had burnt down and my blouse was thin. A deep cold spread throughout my body and tingled in my limbs. "*Free* him?" I repeated. "Bridie, from what must Mr Jamie be freed?"

Her brown eyes, usually so patient, flashed with emotion. Again, she drew a faltering breath. "Miss, d'ye ken the *teind*?"

I kept my voice steady, though my temples throbbed suddenly with painful stabs. "I have heard it mentioned," I told her. "I believe it is a kind of tithe, as farmers pay to the parish, but it is paid to someone else."

"Aye. The *deil*." She lowered her voice, as if speaking such words above a whisper would conjure the Dark Lord himself. "He has Mr Jamie by the throat and willna' leave him be until he goes with his true love. And that be yersel', miss."

There was a constriction in my chest; I could scarcely breathe. Trying to ignore my pounding head, I spoke again. "This payment must be made every seven years, is that correct?"

She nodded gravely.

"It is fourteen years since Mrs Buchanan suffered a severe illness, is it not?"

"Aye, miss."

"And seven years ago, she became so ill she had to leave the castle?"

"He made her try to drown hersel'."

"Who did?

"The *deil*, miss."

"And it is the *deil*, the devil, who has taken her away now. Is that what you mean?"

"Aye."

I laid my hand on her arm. My breath was so short I could hardly speak. I knew of the second, third and fourth *teind*. The question I longed to ask would wait no longer. "Bridie, what happened twenty-one years ago?"

Her watery gaze landed full my face. "Oh, miss, I promised the master I wouldna' tell anyone about it, ever. But I must tell ye, I must, for Mr Jamie's sake!"

She began to cry softly. Her handkerchief useless, her hands remained at her sides while tears slid down her cheeks and dripped off her chin "Miss Lucy was Mrs Buchanan's sister," she whispered. "She died, here at Drumwithie, and so did her wee baby. Now, the *deil* has taken them all."

So the devil had exacted a double tithe. Jamie's assumption had been correct. Lucy had been "ruined" and had given birth to her Frenchman's baby in the tower, where both she and the child died. How terrible for poor Anne, to have to mourn such a loss at a time when she should have been full of joy!

I rose and, sitting beside her on the bed, embraced her. I held her tightly, full of compassion for the loyal servant who had carried this secret knowledge until Anne's death, the latest *teind*, had released her from it.

"I was here," she said, dabbing again at her eyes as we drew apart. "When Miss Lucy and the babe died. It was such a bonny babe. I canna tell ye more."

I wondered why Lucy had returned to Drumwithie. Had she, like any young girl in the final stages of pregnancy, needed her mother?

"Was Mrs McAllister here too?" I asked.

To my surprise, Bridie's eyes widened and she gripped my arm. "No, miss! Dinna mention anything of it to her!"

"Why not?"

"Please, ye promised ye'd no tell anyone." She was near tears again. "Mrs McAllister doesna' ken there ever was a babe!"

Astonished, I could not summon any words. Bridie's imploring look increased in intensity. "And think o' Mr Jamie, will ye, miss? Promise ye'll no leave him!"

I could not make such a promise. To do so and have to go back on my word would be worse than refusing to give it in the first place. "I cannot tell the future, Bridie..." I began, but she interrupted me.

"'Tis in your hands!" she urged. "The spell is wound and only ye can break it!"

I paused, struck by the memory of Jamie's words, that day when I had first told him about the ghost. *The winding of the spell has begun*, he had said, *now you have come*. "And if I do not break the spell?" I asked. "What will happen, Bridie?"

She was agitated enough to grasp both my hands. "The *teinds* will go on, miss. In another seven years, and seven years after that. Nothing else can break the promise made by the faeries to the *deil*. Ye must help us or we'll none of us ever be free of it."

THE HOUR

When I heard the trap pull up the next morning, I rushed downstairs. Bridie, avoiding my eyes, arrived in the hall at the same time.

The doctor had aged in the twenty-four hours since I had last seen him. His pleasant air, which on our first meeting I had taken as his "bedside" manner, and the genial look in his eyes, had gone. He was grey-faced, with a hollow, unseeing expression. Mrs McAllister followed him. She too looked diminished. Her coat and skirt were pulled awkwardly in places; they had been put on without the aid of a lady's maid. Her face was pale and crumpled, and she leaned heavily upon Jamie's arm. Relief flooded through me. The sudden death of his adored mother had not, as I had feared, driven him to collapse.

He shortened his steps to his grandmother's, keeping his eyes down. But his blond lashes flickered minutely as they entered the hall, and I knew he had seen me standing there.

"Catriona, my dear," said the doctor, giving Bridie his hat and stick. He extended his hand to me. "What a neglectful host I have been! But we are home now."

I grasped his hand. "You are very kind, but do not trouble yourself about me. My thoughts are only with you and Jamie and Mrs McAllister. I am so very sorry." I glanced at Bridie, who was gathering Mrs McAllister's cape and Jamie's mackintosh into her arms. "Everyone here is sorry."

"Thank you," said Doctor Hamish. He did not withdraw his hand, but grasped mine tighter and drew it into the crook of his elbow. "Let us go into the Great Hall, where we can talk properly. Could we have some tea, Bridie? I will come to the kitchen and speak to you and MacGregor about Mrs Buchanan later."

Bridie, her face tight with emotion, nodded and curtseyed, and our small procession made its way through the wide doorway into the Great Hall, where Bridie had built an enormous fire. I was grateful that the doctor had not suggested we go into the drawing room, where, however cheerful the fire, Anne Buchanan's portrait would chill the atmosphere. I was sure no one would enter that room for a long time.

Jamie settled Mrs McAllister in her usual fireside chair and his father sat down heavily in the other one, immediately reaching for his silver cigarette case and offering it to Jamie. Surprisingly, Jamie refused. "She always hated people smoking, Father," he said expressionlessly. "I think I'll give it up."

Doctor Hamish struck a match. "Giving it up will be easier for you than for me. Smoking has been my habit for twenty-five years. I doubt if I could ever give it up."

"And why should you?" put in Mrs McAllister. It was a typical interjection, but delivered with more kindness than imperiousness. "If it brings you comfort."

We all fell silent. The doctor smoked thoughtfully, looking into the fire. I was sitting as usual on the footstool, a good position from which to slide a surreptitious glance at Jamie. He had folded himself into the corner of the sofa, his knees, showing bony though the thin material of his trousers, drawn up to his chest. His clothes were those that he had worn while we sorted through the papers from the travelling box, before his father's sudden entrance had changed everything. I had joked that he must have put on whatever garments he had happened to find on the floor of his bedroom that morning: odd socks, the trousers belonging to an old linen suit, the peasant smock I had worn to climb down the glenside.

That flippant remark seemed a long time ago now. Since then, Jamie had worn this hotch-potch of clothes to the hospital, to a smart hotel and, under his mackintosh, on stations and in railway carriages. I imagined the amused comments of passers-by: "Dear me, young people these days!"

I watched him flick his hair back, lean his elbow on the sofa arm and rest his forehead on his hand in the classic pose of the troubled poet. I felt profoundly sorry for him. For the loss of his mother, for the feud with his father, for his uncertain future, and for our imminent parting. Tomorrow I would be on the train south and his grandmother would ensure that we never met again.

"Cat, she killed herself," he said suddenly. He did not change his position, and he was trying to speak without emotion. But his body was tense. I saw the tremor pass through his limbs. "In case you're wondering."

"Oh! Well," I uttered aimlessly. "I—"

"It was that quack's fault!" blurted Jamie, his eyes on his father. "And that horrible hospital! How could they be unaware that she was only taking half her pills, and hiding the others in the *mattress*?"

My heart lurched. Many years ago, Lucy had instructed her sister to hide Matthieu's letters under her mattress. It must have been only a small step from that to finding a weak spot in the seam, ripping it stealthily over several weeks so that the nursing staff did not notice, and secreting pills within the stuffing.

"What sort of place fails to properly search the rooms of suicidal patients?" demanded Jamie. "I told you they could not take care of her and that we should have kept her at home! I *told* you, Father!"

No one spoke. I suspected that Doctor Hamish and Mrs McAllister had already heard Jamie's bewildered protests, perhaps many times.

"Jamie..." I began, "she was grievously ill. And nothing can be done now, after all. The best way to show your love for her is to mourn her, and leave her in the peace she evidently sought."

This did not come out exactly the way I might have wished, but Jamie did not turn on me in anger. He took his hand away from his forehead and looked at me, his eyes fully open and his face in repose. "Well said," he murmured. "But what of *my* peace?"

I returned his look. Both of us knew that Jamie could have no peace until the mystery of Lucy McAllister was solved. I longed to tell him what Bridie had said, and my own conclusions about the *teind* his family had been compelled to pay for so many years. But I could do no more than I had already done; the path to the truth lay in other hands. "You must achieve it as best you can," I said gently, hoping he understood my message. "It is up to you."

Mrs McAllister raised her head. "What are you muttering, you two? And where is that tea? Hamish, ring the bell."

"There is no need," the doctor assured her. "Bridie will not neglect her duties, though the house is in mourning. Which reminds me, we must all change before luncheon. Jamie, will you put on your best suit for now? We shall go to the tailor's next week and get you some proper mourning." He threw his cigarette butt into the fire. "There can be no funeral until the procurator has made his ruling, which may be two weeks or more. The inquest will almost certainly find that she took her own life while in unsound mind, and we may bury her in the Buchanan grave in Drumwithie church-yard. Until then, and for a few weeks afterwards, we must dress in deep mourning."

So Anne's resting place would be here at Drumwithie. Where, I wondered, did her sister's body lie?

Bridie brought the tea while Doctor Hamish was speaking. She had resumed the invisibility of a servant, but I noticed the smudges of sleeplessness under her eyes. Looking at no one, she closed the door silently behind her and we busied ourselves with tea.

Unexpectedly, Mrs McAllister addressed me. "Well, Catriona, what are we to do with you? Hamish will write and tell your mother of our bereavement. I am sure she would like to attend Mrs Buchanan's funeral, as Hamish attended her husband's. And so will you, of course. But meanwhile, perhaps you would be better off at home?"

"No!" exclaimed Jamie, with such vigour he almost upset his tea. "She is staying here, with me!" He put down the cup and saucer with a gesture of irritation, and, sliding forward on the sofa cushion, reached out for my hand. "What is the point of Cat going back to Oxfordshire or Warwickshire or wherever it is, only to come all the way back with her mother for the funeral? And anyway, I need her beside me. We have things to do, have we not, Cat?"

Mrs McAllister took in breath to speak, but was prevented by Doctor Hamish, who was looking curiously from Jamie to me and back again. It was a relief to see the return of the usual intelligent expression in his eyes. "What things?" he asked. "Are you two plotting something?"

I hesitated and glanced at Jamie. Fired with sudden energy,

he sprang up and pulled me with him. "*We* are not plotting anything, Father," he declared, "but *someone* is!"

Everyone stared at him. "Jamie!" I warned. "Take care!"

But his eyes were alight. "It is here, Cat!" he cried. "The hour is come!"

He was right. There was no more need for concealment. Anne Buchanan was beyond the reach of earthly sorrow, and Lucy's desire for the truth to be revealed could not be clearer. "Say it, then," I told him. "Ask your questions. She is listening."

"*Who* is listening?" asked Mrs McAllister, her teacup cradled in her gloved hands, her eyes full of distrust.

Jamie turned to his grandmother. She was sitting, he was standing; her head in its wide-brimmed hat was tilted towards his face. In that moment, I thought how alike they looked, and how alike they *were*. Uncompromising in their opinions, fierce in their loyalty, passionate in their enthusiasms. "*Lucy* is listening," said Jamie.

His words fell into silence and lay there like stones. Jamie's fingers entwined themselves with mine, our knuckles pressing against each other. Knowing he sought my support, I returned his grip.

"What do *you* know of Lucy?" It was the doctor. He did not sound angry or suspicious; he spoke calmly. Affection for him rose in me. *He* was the one, I realized in a flash of understanding, who would enlighten us at last.

Jamie faced him squarely. "Lucy McAllister was my aunt.

246

She was Grandmother's younger daughter, Mother's sister. Cat and I went into the cave and found the box. We know that she ran away, more than twenty years ago, to meet a Frenchman."

I heard Mrs McAllister gasp, and her teacup fell from her hand. Hot tea spilled over her skirt, but she took no notice. "What utter nonsense! Hamish, tell them they are quite wrong!"

But the doctor did not reply to her. "What cave?" he asked Jamie. "What box?"

"The cave that was inaccessible for so long, Father. On the glenside. The slide moved the tree, and we got in. There was a box hidden there, full of papers about Lucy. And photographs. Your wedding photograph. Why have you kept Lucy a secret all these years?"

Mrs McAllister had risen and was standing before the fire, holding the corner of the mantelpiece for support. Her face was red and her chin trembled. She gave her son-in-law a look full of meaning. My conviction that the doctor held the key to the mystery increased. But I, meanwhile, was in possession of some information no one knew I had.

"Doctor, if I may…"

"What do you wish to say, Catriona?" He had remained sitting in the fireside chair; as I stood there beside Jamie, I was looking down on him. I could see the balding spot on the crown of his head, and was reminded of my father, whose hair had thinned in exactly the same place.

"I know that Lucy had a baby, but it died."

Mrs McAllister uttered a shocked cry, almost a shriek. Her hand went to her throat. "Lucy never had a baby!" she declared breathlessly. "Do you not think her own mother would have known if she did? The suggestion is outrageous, and I insist you take it back, Miss Catriona!"

Doctor Hamish's head snapped back and he stared stonily up at me. "How the devil can you know this, child?"

"Cat, what is going on?" asked Jamie almost at the same time.

I felt very awkward. "Perhaps you are aware, Doctor, that someone else in the house knows the secret," I said. "And, in view of recent events, you will not blame that person for betraying it."

"But I don't understand!" complained Jamie. "We know Lucy ran away and we know she died. But there was nothing in that box about a baby, and my grandmother denies there ever was one!"

"And I say again, there was not!" cried Mrs McAllister. "You are my only grandchild, Jamie, dead or alive!"

Doctor Hamish lowered his head and sighed. It was a long, shuddering, soul-shaking sigh. The sigh of a man cornered, exhausted, and no longer able to fight. In it I heard twenty-one years of pent-up lies, secrets and pretence, stretched to breaking-point. The hour had indeed come.

"If you please, Jean," he said to his mother-in-law, "sit down. I wish you to listen to what I have to say. It will

248

distress you, for which I am sorry. But I cannot bear this burden any longer. Now that Anne is gone and these young people have discovered Lucy's existence, there is no point in this charade any more. I will confess the truth."

Mrs McAllister was very near to tears. I felt profoundly sorry for her. To have lost her husband and both her daughters was tragic enough, but to have had a grandchild she knew nothing about, and who had also died, was truly affecting. She sat down. Removing her hat, she rested her head against the back of the chair, and waited. Jamie, his body rigid with expectation, remained standing, his hand still locked in mine. My thoughts filled with Lucy: her bedraggled pink dress, the beseeching look in her eyes, her youth and fragility. She could not be present in the room, and yet she was.

"When Lucy disappeared, just before Christmas 1887," began the doctor, "it was to elope with a Frenchman. I do not recall his name."

"His name was Matthieu de Villiers," said Mrs McAllister unsteadily. "I found letters, after Lucy had gone away. It was I who put them in the box."

"But when she returned," continued Doctor Hamish, "it was not quite as you think, Jean. She came back a few days before I told you she had. On 25th January 1889, in fact – the day Jamie was born You were away at the time, visiting your friend Mrs Seddon, in Yorkshire."

Mrs McAllister nodded distractedly. "I have not thought about Eliza Seddon for years," she murmured.

Jamie's grasp on my hand had relaxed. Slowly, feeling for the sofa behind him, he sat down. He did not take his eyes from his father's face. I lowered myself beside him, ready to do whatever he wished.

"That night," said the doctor, staring into nothing, seeing his memories, "the weather was wet. It had been raining for days; the ground was sodden. Anne, who was in the late stages of pregnancy, was resting in her drawing room while I worked in the library. I had been concerned for several hours that her pains were beginning, so I preferred her to remain near me rather than go to bed. About seven o'clock, she called to me to say she thought she had heard something, a noise at the window. I tried to calm her, but she insisted I go out to see what it was. It was Burns Night; MacGregor was at the pub in the village, Bridie was in the kitchen. I assumed Anne had heard a bird fly into the windowpane, or some such thing, but I was wrong.

"On the ground beneath the drawing-room window, soaked through, sat Lucy. She was half dead with cold and hunger, wearing only a silk gown and a thin cape." His eyes flicked to my face, but there was no accusation or hostility in them. "You are correct, Catriona, she was about to have a child. Her time was very near, so I did not wait for an explanation, but carried her indoors, wrapped her in a blanket and laid her in the tower bedroom. You see, Bridie was at that time sleeping in the small room next to the room that is now Jamie's, in case Anne needed her in the night, and Lucy did not wish her to hear anything. As you know, the tower room is far away from the other bedrooms, and has the thickest walls. Lucy implored me to deliver her child there and have it taken away immediately. She was so ashamed, she did not wish you, Jean, or anyone else, to know of the baby."

"In that, then, she succeeded," said Mrs McAllister faintly.

The doctor looked at her bleakly. "But I was less expert in obstetrics than I am now. As I had feared, Anne's time came upon her that same night, and I could not manage the labours of two women at the same time, especially since Anne's proved a difficult one. So I had to swear Bridie to secrecy and beg her assistance."

"And what of MacGregor?" asked Mrs McAllister. "Does he know that my daughter gave birth in the tower room?"

"Aye. It was not until the next day that she died. But he and Bridie promised faithfully never to speak of it."

They had kept that promise. They had spoken of the events of that night only to each other, until now.

"When you came back from Mrs Seddon's, Jean," continued the doctor, "you will recall I met you with the terrible news that Lucy had returned, but had died of a fever. I had by that time signed her death certificate, and had it counter-signed by Doctor Skerran, who was a young man then, and very busy with his practice in Dunkeith. He did not come over to examine Lucy's body. Forgive me" – his voice shook – "but I did not tell you the exact truth. Lucy *did* die of a fever, but a particular kind of fever, that afflicts women who have just given birth. It came on in the early hours. Anne, who had also just given birth, was sleeping deeply. And so was I."

He pinched the bridge of his nose, his face full of regret. "I wish I had *not* been," he said softly. "I wish Lucy had not lain in the tower, so far away from our bedroom. But I was exhausted. If she cried out, I did not hear her. Poor Lucy had some hours of delirium, during which I did everything I could, but she fell into unconsciousness and died the next day."

Mrs McAllister was weeping openly. Without her hat she appeared smaller, and I noticed that her hair was coming loose at the nape of her neck. "Oh, Hamish, how could you not tell me she had a child, when even the servants knew?" she wailed. "Even though it did not live, how could you keep it from me?"

There was a pause. I could hear Jamie's breathing and Mrs McAllister's soft sobs. Then Hamish spoke in a steady voice. "We must go back to that Burns Night, when both Anne and Lucy gave birth to their babies. Lucy's was born at eleven o'clock, and Anne's half an hour afterwards." He put his head in his hands. His words were indistinct, but audible. "And this is where you are wrong, Catriona. It was not Lucy's son that never drew breath. It was Anne's."

Jamie was still. Absolutely still, like a statue. His grandmother's features were blanketed by shock.

Tears came to the doctor's eyes, but did not fall. "When I

told Lucy that my son had died, she begged us to take you, Jamie, and bring you up as our son. She insisted that you should never know she existed. 'Do not tell him,' she said, 'I will go back to Paris. I would rather give him to you than have him brought up by strangers.'" He sighed deeply. "Those were the last words she spoke, except in the distraction of her fever. And so we did as she asked. Anne and I buried our son in Blairguthrie's woods. The spot is not marked. From that moment on we pretended you were ours, Jamie. And Lucy's wish was granted. By then, death had taken her. You and she never met."

It was true, Jamie had never met his mother. But I had. My presence in the room where she had died had summoned her. I had heard her screams and the shrieking of the crows that encircled the tower while she fought with delirium and death. I had seen her, still clad in the dress she had made her way home in, and which she was wearing when she died. In her labour or her illness there had been no time for the niceties of nursing. Her brother-in-law had tended with all his skill, but had failed to save her. Perhaps, years later, by saving the lives of other women and babies, he was still trying to atone for her loss.

The doctor had raised his head and was looking at Jamie anxiously. "I cannot expect your forgiveness, my dearest son, but I hope you understand the depth of our love for you. Anne adored you as you adored her. You were our son in every way but the biological one. And even so, you were

Anne's blood relation, her nephew. And of course, you have always been your grandmother's true grandson."

Jamie said nothing. I could not look at him.

"You have your grandmother's eyes," said Doctor Hamish. "Lucy was dark like Anne, but your French father was, by Lucy's account, golden-haired. When she saw you, she expressed the hope that you would be fair like him."

Jamie, the golden-haired changeling. The faerie child left for another.

The *teind* to the devil, to repay for the sins of signing an inaccurate death certificate, and burying an unregistered child.

How Anne must have suffered! The summer before Jamie's birth, my father had visited Drumwithie. Had she fallen in love with him? Had it been another golden-haired child she carried – my father's? Clearly, her mother suspected as much. Thinking Jamie to be my half-brother, Mrs McAllister had tried to warn me from him, not with the truth – she could never disclose such shameful suspicions – but with snobbishness and contempt.

I could hardly bring myself to imagine Anne's torment. The nightmare of giving birth to a stillborn son, burying him in secret and losing her sister. Perfectly healthy before, she had been robbed of her peace, and gradually, her sanity. Now, in the final payment, she had died by her own hand. And in doing so, she had revealed the truths that had been hidden for so long. Mrs McAllister now knew her daughters' secrets and Jamie knew that Doctor Hamish was not his father. But Hamish had always known of his son's parentage, and still forced him down the path of medicine. The man whose hand I held, whose arm I could feel through his sleeve, whose narrow thigh lay partly covered by my skirt as we sat together among the sofa cushions, was the son of a passionate seventeen-year-old girl and Matthieu de Villiers, a French artist about whom all we knew was his name.

According to the faerie legend, the seven-yearly *teind* would be broken only when the changeling child found his true love. And I, the outsider, the faerie presence whom Lucy had begged to stay in the room where she had died, and whom Bridie had begged not to leave Jamie, had not fallen in love with my half-brother at all. My half-brother, if he was such, lay in an anonymous grave in the woods beyond the glen.

It was the next day. Jamie and I were lying on our backs in a storm-flattened clearing among the gorse bushes. The sun was out and beat on our faces with welcome, increasingly ferocious heat. We had covered the damp ground with the blanket from Jamie's sofa.

"Are you happy?" he asked me.

His eyes were closed, his face serene. His hair, now in even greater need of cutting, fell away from his forehead. He looked young and sweet, like a child with no experience of the sadness of the world.

"Happier than I have the right to be," I told him.

"Everyone has the right to be happy."

I doubted this, though I did not say so. "But it is hard not to feel guilty about being happy, when so many *un*happy things have happened."

He did not speak or open his eyes, but I could tell by the miniscule movement of his eyebrows that he was interested.

"For instance," I went on, "when you first said that you cared for me, I was so happy I wanted to dance all over the castle, shouting for joy. During those wonderful days, I simply did not understand how I could feel such happiness when my father had passed away only a month before."

I was looking at him sideways, noticing the shape of his nose as it pointed at the sky, and the shadow of his lashes on his sun-reddened skin. He still said nothing.

"I loved my father so much, Jamie!" I turned my head back to face the sun and closed my own eyes. "And yet within such a short time, I have found someone new to love. How can that be, that you can love someone with all your heart, yet at the same time give that heart to someone else?"

"It is easy," he said. "I too have done it, and my mother – that is, the woman who brought me up as her son – is only two days in her coffin."

I took his hand and we lay there, enclosed in the secret, selfish world of love. Him. Me. Our hands touching. The woollen blanket beneath our heads, the warmth of the sun, our unshakeable conviction of each other's devotion. I rolled over and laid my head on his chest. My blouse collar began to stick to my neck and my hair grew damp. My cheek was very warm against Jamie's shirt, but I did not move. If time could stand still, at least for those few minutes, the moment of parting, when he would set off for Edinburgh, and I for Gilchester, could be postponed, and postponed…

"It is too hot out here now. I must go in the shade," said Jamie at last. With his usual decisiveness he disentangled himself and jumped to his feet. "And I must speak to my father. Get up."

"What do you wish to speak to him about?" I asked as we folded the blanket.

"Something very important." He gazed intently into my face, the blanket in his arms, his eyes alight and alert. "Do you honestly think you are going to go back to Bilchester or Dimchester or whatever it's called, to sit at home and wait? For what? For some ghastly pen-pusher, probably wearing a monocle, to appear and pass your mother's inspection?"

He set off towards the house. I followed him, trying to keep up, stumbling through the long grass. "But you are going away!"

I could not help it. My voice cracked. Thinking about parting was painful enough, but speaking of it was much worse.

Jamie stopped, turned and stared at me. "I will never leave you, Cat," he said sternly. "Ever."

I did not understand. What declaration was he making?

That he wished me to stay at Drumwithie? That he intended to stay at Drumwithie himself and not go to study in Edinburgh at all?

"Wait for me," I begged. "I am too hot and I cannot keep up with you!"

He waited at the bridge. When I was by his side he put his arm around my waist and we entered the house. The vestibule was cool, and so dark after the brightness outside, I could hardly see where I trod. Jamie tossed the blanket onto a chair and opened the door to the hall. Its high window threw an oblong of sunlight onto the flagstones. At the bottom of the stairs, with her hand on the banister-post, stood Mrs McAllister.

She was hatless; her hair, done in the old-fashioned style with a mass of curls at the front, was still a rich chestnut colour, with only a few streaks of grey. She was dressed in a loose house gown. Last night, Doctor Hamish had refused to allow her to be alone at the Lodge, so she was staying at Drumwithie. She had risen late and had not put on her corset. I suspected that such things as deportment, formal attire and disapproval of modern girls' behaviour had diminished in importance. But now she had been robbed, albeit temporarily, of her strict demeanour, I was much more inclined to like her.

Her green eyes, dulled by grief and sleeplessness, studied Jamie's face. She did not hold her hand out for him to kiss. "Where is my box?" she asked.

Jamie went to her side. "How are you this morning, Grandmother? Do you wish to sit down?"

"Where is my box?" she repeated.

"It is still in the cave," he said, with a glance at me. "But the papers are not inside it. They are upstairs in my sitting room. We have not yet finished looking through them."

"Retrieve the box," said Mrs McAllister calmly, "and put the letters back in it. There is no need to look through any more of them. It is finished. Lucy is dead, and buried with her father in the churchyard of St Matthew's, though her name is not on the headstone. I could not even grant her that dignity, may God forgive me."

Jamie hesitated. "Grandmother," he said with a sideways glance at me, "may we ask why you put the photographs and letters in the box, and hid it?"

Mrs McAllister sighed. "I was ashamed that Lucy had run away and lived in sin with that man. I was indignant that she had put him before me, and Anne, and everything she knew. I had always encouraged her in her artistic endeavours – I even took her to London to try to sell her paintings. It was hardly *my* fault that no one bought them." She paused, and looked at Jamie sorrowfully. "But I could not bear to destroy these things after she died, as they were all I had left of her. It was a very good hiding place, was it not?"

"Yes," agreed Jamie. "And even better when the oak tree fell and blocked the entrance."

Mrs McAllister's chin began to wobble and she took a

lace-trimmed handkerchief from her pocket. "That was a gift from God!" she said, wiping her eyes. "But what God giveth, He taketh away. When MacGregor came in the other day and said the land had slid again, I prayed the tree would not be dislodged. But God knows best."

Neither Jamie nor I spoke; there seemed nothing to say that would comfort her. She wept for a few moments, then, as she began to recover, her eyes fell on me. With a faint smile, she addressed me. "You are dark like Lucy was, Catriona. She even had a similar shape of eye, though yours have quite a different expression. As for your figure and your way of moving, you are quick and light like she was. Never still, always wanting to be outdoors, unless she was bent over one of her drawings. A creature from another world, my husband used to say, quite unlike Anne, who was quiet and all too human." She thought for a moment, the smile fading. "Though Anne, it must be said, had the greater share of beauty."

"A creature from another world," repeated Jamie. He fixed me with his green gaze. "Our Cait Sìth, who came from the faeries to find Lucy for me." His eyes slid to Mrs McAllister. "Do you not agree, Grandmother, that without Cat none of this would have happened? I would still be unaware that I am a changeling, and not at all who I thought I was."

Embarrassed, I began to make apologies to Mrs McAllister. But she interrupted me. "I do agree. There *is* something of the faeries about you, Catriona, as there was about Lucy. And the power of the faeries is great, though in this modern world, many deny it. They have our human lives, and deaths, in their grasp."

She paused and tilted her head towards Jamie. "So you will return the letters to the box, my dear?"

I had never heard her use a term of endearment towards her grandson before. "Of course, Grandmother," he said. Then something occurred to him. "But may I keep the photographs? Of my mother in her best dress? And the wedding?"

She bowed her permission in her gracious way. "And now, I had better get dressed. We shall meet again this evening."

She began to climb the stairs, a mass of figured crêpe de Chine billowing in her wake, and her loose sleeves floating at her wrists. Jamie and I watched her in silence until she disappeared around the corner of the landing.

"What are you so anxious to speak to your father about?" I asked him again.

He gave me a bemused look. "About you. You are the only loose end left."

"I am not a loose end!" I said, offended. "What nonsense you talk!"

"You are so impatient," he said, putting his arms around me. "You must wait and see."

After supper the doctor suggested we take our coffee outside into the garden. Jamie helped Bridie fetch the wrought-iron table and chairs, and we settled ourselves on the west-facing lawn.

The evening light was glorious in itself, but as it fell on the castle walls it was an especially beautiful sight, burnishing the stone to grey–gold, and the windows to jewels. The sky was as pink as a silk petticoat above the refreshed greens of the glen. And in the distance lay the blue mountains. Drumwithie stood, square and shining, as it always had.

In Doctor Hamish's eyes the haunted look of last night had given way to the fatigue of a long day. But he was calm. Mrs McAllister looked drawn and seemed loath to talk, and there were shadows under Jamie's eyes. As they drank their coffee in quiet contemplation, in all their faces I saw the bewilderment that sudden bereavement brings.

All evening I had been possessed of a restlessness unlike any I had ever known. My heartbeat would not settle. It murmured unnervingly, as if in anticipation of something unknown. I had eaten so little supper the doctor had been concerned, but my stomach seemed to be in the wrong place, much higher up than usual, and I had found it impossible to swallow.

I put down my coffee cup and gathered my skirt. "It is such a lovely evening, I think I'll go for a walk," I announced, to no one in particular.

None of them moved to accompany me; each seemed preoccupied. I was anxious to exercise my limbs and hoped the view of the valley would calm me. I stood up, meaning to set off in the direction of Anne's garden. But I had not taken two steps before the doctor spoke again. "Catriona, my dear, do not leave us."

I stopped beside his chair. He took hold of my arm lightly. "I would like to speak with you about something, and I fear I will not get the chance again for a while." He paused, weighing his words. "I must go to Edinburgh tomorrow, for several days, and I do not wish you, or anyone else, to make any hasty decisions in my absence."

I waited uncertainly. What decisions did he mean?

"About the future," he continued. He felt for the silver cigarette case, took out a cigarette and tapped it absentmindedly on the lid. I watched, seeing my father's fingers doing the same thing, on the same cigarette case. "*Your* future, Catriona. Do you have any thoughts on the matter?"

I could not get my breath. I fumbled for an answer. "I expect I will go home to Mother."

"Indeed." The cigarette remained unlit between the doctor's fingers. He fixed me with his steady, sensible, doctor's gaze. "So you are still of a mind to do what you described to us: stay at Chester House until you are married and eventually inherit Graham's Wholesome Foods?" he asked.

I turned and looked at Jamie. I could not help myself. He responded with a cool, inscrutable gaze. Mrs McAllister, who had closed her eyes, opened then again. I turned back to face the doctor. "Well…" I ventured uncertainly, then stopped. I did not know what to say.

"Or will you allow me to present you with an alternative suggestion?" he asked. "One that I can take only partial credit for, but have been charged with imparting to you?"

I nodded, silenced by expectation. Though he was sitting where I could not see him, I sensed Jamie's expectation too.

"I am convinced," continued the doctor, "and I would very easily convince your dear mother that you would never be comfortable in the life she envisages for you. I believe Miss Catriona Graham would rather be educated and free to enter a profession that admits women, the number of which is growing every year. Am I right?"

My mouth fell open. I closed it again, my brain racing. But I had no breath to make a reply. I must have been staring at the doctor as if he had gone mad. I managed a nod, but that was all.

"Very well," he said with satisfaction. He struck a match and lit his cigarette at last. "Then I will leave Jamie to tell you of the plan we have been hatching," he said, blowing out the first puff of smoke. "I can see he is itching to do so."

"Behold Miss Graham, future student of the University of Edinburgh!" came Jamie's voice from behind me.

I spun round, still too astonished to speak. His face was full of what I could only describe as many kinds of light. The light of the setting sun, the light of joy, and the light of love.

"Will you stay here at Drumwithie with us?" he asked. "And be tutored by Father and others, perhaps my old tutors – the mathematics chap was pretty good – in preparation for the examinations? *You* will go to the University too. And Father will get his wish of not leaving Drumwithie in the hands of a wastrel, because what is mine, my dearest Cat, will be yours."

I went on standing there, in the landscape yellowed by the lowering sun. Jamie, his father and his grandmother went on sitting in the garden chairs, with the coffee pot cooling on the table and the smoke from the doctor's cigarette making blue curls in the still air. This moment, when such unimaginable happiness descended upon me, seemed suspended in space, as immoveable as a star.

"Oh, thank you, thank you!" I blurted. My heart was pounding so hard I had to put my hands over it. I felt tears sting my eyelids. "I am so happy … I cannot express… Jamie, this is so wonderful!"

He came and stood beside me, and the golden sun fell on his golden hair. "It is you, our Cait Sìth sent from the faeries, who have made this happiness," he said. "Mine, my father's, my own." He glanced at his grandmother, who raised her eyebrows and nodded at me. "You see, even Grandmother, who can scarcely believe there *are* any professional women, approves." He took my hands in both of his. "She loves you as we all do, darling Cat."

I clasped his hands tightly. He drew me towards him and kissed me on each cheek. "Catriona Graham, I gave you my promise once that I would love and care for you always," he said solemnly. "Well, I still hold to that promise."

"And I promise too." My voice was shaky. "James Buchanan, I will love and care for you always."

It was a betrothal, though an unconventional one. The doctor and Mrs McAllister rose and shook our hands, and we stood there in the lengthening shadow of the castle walls until the sun had disappeared below the mountains, and Drumwithie was in darkness again.

Ten days later

"This is the place."

Doctor Hamish prodded the earth with his stick. Jamie and I stood beside him, breathless from our climb through Blairguthrie's woods. Though autumn would soon be upon us, the weather was warm and humid. But I could not take off my hat or coat. It would not be respectful to the memory of the person we had come to honour.

Jamie stepped forward and laid a small brass plaque upon the ground. We all looked at it, set there on a mossy, leaf-strewn patch of earth that was too shaded from the sunlight for any grass to grow. It had not been possible to engrave it with the usual sort of epitaph for a child, because this burial had been illegal and must remain secret. Instead, it bore one word only: *Cat.*

It had been Jamie's idea. If anyone should chance upon the plaque, he had declared, they would assume it marked the burial place of a beloved pet. Mrs McAllister had approved; it had been a cat, of sorts, that had brought her second grandson back to her.

"The soil is loose here," observed Doctor Hamish. His voice was serious, but not distressed. "We knew these woods so well, Anne and I, it was easy for us to find a convenient spot."

I thought how different the place must have been on that long-ago January day. The treetops had perhaps been agitated by the wind, or sleet had fallen in freezing spikes that stung the faces of the man and the woman as they lowered their baby into his grave. And the enormity of the secret they had kept for all these years struck me once again: if Lucy had not been so strictly bound by an unforgiving society's rules, she would never have given up her child. Jamie would have grown up at the Lodge with his mother and grandmother, and gone to school like other boys. Anne might never have become ill, and another boy might have been born to her. This little boy and his cousin, like Hamish Buchanan and David Graham before them, would have grown to love Drumwithie, spending happy days in this wild and beautiful landscape.

But society's rules could not be broken. I wondered ruefully if the twenty-one years that had passed had changed those rules at all. New Georgians we might be, and women might achieve the vote and enter professions, as Doctor Hamish predicted. But if I were to have a baby without a husband, would my own mother welcome me and my child to Chester House and brave the social stigma of such a scandalous event? I doubted it.

I shuddered, violently enough for Jamie to step closer and draw my arm around his waist. Doctor Hamish's eyes were closed; I wondered if he was praying. His brow was not furrowed or his mouth drawn. He looked at peace.

All around us was silence. I gazed down at my name, alert for a sound which never came. No birds sang; no leaves rustled. And high above, where the trees met the sky, no crows' wings beat their death knell. They no longer held the power to herald disaster. The master of Drumwithie, his heir, his family and those who served them, were free.

THE END

*"I saw no one but him, dreaming or waking.
I fell in love so madly, I almost did not recognize it as love.
It was madness and nothing else."*

The story of Mary Wollstonecraft and Percy Bysshe Shelley
is one of the most famous love stories of all time
– passionate yet volatile, heart-warming yet heart-breaking
– and the backdrop to the writing of the world-famous
novel Frankenstein.

"Those in search of a good story need look no further."
The Guardian

"A haunting story, beautifully written and rich
in historical detail." *The Bookseller*